After earning degrees in philosophy at Catholic University of America, Washington, DC, and California State University, San Francisco, Lawrence Boesch worked as a fundraiser for public interest groups for over three years, before attending Golden Gate University School of Law, from which he graduated in May 1983.

Lawrence practiced civil litigation in the Bay Area for 28 years (1986–2014) before relocating his practice to Southern California, where he worked for law firms in Century City, Calabasas, Beverly Hills, Torrance, and Long Beach.

On his retirement in May 2022, he returned to San Jose, California, where he enjoys the company of his wife, two sons and their wives, and two grandchildren.

For those who have found the straight and narrow path too
slick to avoid treacherous encounters.

Lawrence Boesch

RELUCTANT HERO

AUSTIN MACAULEY PUBLISHERS™

LONDON • CAMBRIDGE • NEW YORK • SHARJAH

Ordering Information
Quantity sales: Special discounts are available on quantity purchases by corporations, associations, and others. For details, contact the publisher at the address below.

Publisher's Cataloging-in-Publication data
Boesch, Lawrence
Reluctant Hero

ISBN 9798889104636 (Paperback)
ISBN 9798889104643 (ePub e-book)

Library of Congress Control Number: 2023918426

www.austinmacauley.com/us

First Published 2024
Austin Macauley Publishers LLC
40 Wall Street, 33rd Floor, Suite 3302
New York, NY 10005
USA

mail-usa@austinmacauley.com
+1 (646) 5125767

The author acknowledges the Catholic University Athletic Department for their tolerance of his experimental techniques, the San Jose, California Police Department for its training in the Citizens Academy, and his wife, Keiko, for the support necessary to enable this book to come to fruition.

Table of Contents

Pars Uno

Chapter 1
The Landscape

It was Christmas Eve when Bernie, the stocky stout ornament, was placed on the bottom bough of the newly-decorated tree. The other ornaments, flashy and dusty simultaneously, snubbed him, thinking that the new kid on the block needed to get a few celebrations under his belt before advancing to a front bough.

For Bernie's part, he had already been through quite enough, thank you. He had suffered the furnace heat of the manufacturer, had glue attaching sparkles and tinsel to his exterior, had been fitted and refitted for a horse collar, and finally, had been painted with a disgusting smelling, sticky orange substance.

Bernie knew that his destiny was to shine through many Christmas seasons to come. He desired the opportunity to reflect the darling glow from the bubbly tree lights, or to show the face of innocents peering into the tree with packages laid neatly below.

But he was resigned to his fate—temporarily—having to wait his turn to sit nearer the star at the top, or even on a branch-tip closest to the most cumbersome decorations, like the cardboard train, the yarn Santa, or even, dare he strive for it, within a baby's breath of the photo of Greg, the red bell or the plastic snowperson.

Bernie felt the scorn of his fellow ornaments about as long as they had warned him that his situation was precarious. Bernie saw the 50s style reddish-delicate bulb hit the floor in an unceremonious demise.

He saw the string of lights left in the box, and he saw the multi-colored ornaments left untouched in the box, awaiting their entry unto a secondary choice back-up tree, in case the primary one was insufficient to lighten up the flat by itself.

Meanwhile, Artie, the forgotten John Fitzgerald Kennedy white rose, sweated in the plastic wrapper in which she had been stored since November. She did not know that she was to be planted in the front yard.

Chauncey, the long-standing icicle chain, was repugnant as he saw Master John lining up the stepladder to take him down. It was nearing sundown. Doesn't that fidgety human ever give himself a break? How could he change exterior lights this time of day, with the holiday fast approaching?

Chauncey had been the long-standing anchor for the outdoor Christmas lights, but his flicker wasn't as bright as it had been when he was fresh-out-of-the-box. MJ had watched the light strings above the front door fade and ultimately die out. One of them was new, so it had to be a bad connection.

Chauncey knew that the place above the doorway was a vaunted location by many perspectives, but he had always been the first lights to be seen as people turned the corner into the cul-de-sac. He wanted that to be his legacy, when the last current flowed through his wires.

Artie, Bernie, and Chauncey were destined for things different than their limited imaginations at that time might have perceived.

The next day, as the sun rose above the houses to the East, Artie looked around self-consciously to see her new neighbors. Having been planted just before dusk on Christmas Eve, she felt a certain celebrity, until she saw her closest neighbor, the blood-red rose planted on Mother's Day five years ago, and behind him, the two grandmas of the yard, pink rose bush I and pink rose bush II, whose stems grew seven feet tall before blossoming.

Artie thought it better to hold her peace, at least until one of them spoke first. Then, when Blood-Red cleared his throat and spoke, it was not of the grand scheme of things, but rather of the shortest bush in the yard, the delicately-balanced lavender bush who had struggled for three years to establish and maintain a foothold on the slope to the northeast of the Blood-Red. It had been planted at an angle in the shadow of the junipers.

"Lavvie wants to say 'Hello' but he's blocked by my big branches," BR said.

"Oh, well, I can't really see him from here," Artie replied, "but if he's anywhere near as stately as the lemon-yellow just outside your shadow, I'm betting he's gorgeous."

"Well, he's a she," Blood-Red laughed.

"And flattery will get you everywhere," chimed in the Yellow Rose on the perch just beside the driveway.

Chapter 2
Christmas Night

That sundown, Artie was adjusting to the temperature change between the warmth of the sawdust-packed wrapping inside the container that had kept her warm for weeks, and the cold, wet ground, packed with topsoil that was dirty and nasty. She couldn't believe that this was her destiny, to be planted in the ground, like a common weed. With a breeding like the Fitzgerald Kennedy-branch, she assumed that she'd be planted in a warm southern climate within the courtyard of a prestigious judicial chamber.

She kept her head and branches withdrawn, to maximize what little comfort she would gather.

Suddenly, when she was getting drowsy, she looked up to see a bright light peering through the branches of the tall redwood tree. The little bush hadn't noticed the star's arrival. The light was almost like a spotlight announcing the appearance of a star. She blushed as much as the white color of her buds would permit.

Voices down the street, beyond the sisterly pinks, shattered the peaceful quiet. One said, "Are you sure?"

The other replied, "Yeah, we did a Google-search!"

"Well, what does it take to flush him out?" The first voice asked.

"My bet is that the younger generation shows up any minute," said the second.

Little did they know that Master John's sons had chosen that Christmas to spend abroad, leaving John and his wife, Mary, to themselves that evening. The men were in for a long, uninterrupted stake-out.

The voices discussed their game-plan. One said, "Do you have enough ammunition?"

The other responded, "You? What do you mean 'You'?"

"Well, it was just a figure of speech!" The first said, a little agitated.

Artie wondered why the voices didn't arouse the other roses in their beds. She reasoned that, if they stirred at every human voice that drifted over them, they would constantly be in a state of agitation—not a healthy prospect for fragile vegetation.

Then, the orange rose, hidden by the yellow one, beyond Artie's sight, whispered, "I don't care, as long as he doesn't bring out those infernal pruning shears!"

Artie shuddered. She had heard about the gardeners' pruning, as the leaves drop and the first chills of oncoming winter set in. She hated to think that someday, her lovely limbs would also be so brutally chapped.

"Well, you should be concerned," said the lavender bush between the yellow and the Blood-Red. This was the first time Artie heard Lavvie's voice; it surprised her greatly. The voice was unlike the masculine Blood-Red or the Yellow Rose's soft voice.

"He feeds us, waters us, fertilizes our ground, keeps the nasty insects off us, and cuts the blossoms before they decay!" Lavvie continued.

"Well, we should mind our own business," chirped in Blood-Red, whom Artie thought to be slumbering. "What could we do, anyway?" He intoned, as he seemed about to resume his sleep.

Suddenly from the front steps came a gravelly voice, "Pipe down there, you stupid plants!" It was Chauncey, the venerable icicle Christmas lights, about which even the newcomer Artie knew the scuttlebutt. Chauncey was beyond aging gracefully, was positively out of style, and likely to be replaced once and for all by new bulbs.

The roses fluttered their little leaves, but felt too intimidated to speak up until one, whose voice Artie did not recognize, responded, "Oh, pipe down yourself, you cantankerous old electric appliance!" From the direction of the voice, Artie determined it must have been one of the pinks. Little did she know, but the pink roses always spoke together, being of one mind.

Chapter 3
Alert

A hush fell over the front yard as the door opened and Master John appeared. The boys out in front were aghast and ran off. John looked around quizzically, trying to determine the source of all this murmuring.

The only thing missing from the scene was snow. In central California, the yard had probably only seen snow once in the past century. The mischievous souls who had been talking moments ago were now back in their vehicle, but not going anywhere. The pinks, the orange rose, and the Yellow Rose resolved among themselves to take turns watching them.

A few hours later, the vehicle's door opened, and the younger lad emerged. "I'm not waiting any longer. I want to get the show on the road." He was carrying a double-barreled shotgun, and was apparently not in a good mood.

The older one started the engine. He was not waiting to see how things developed. As he raised the gun to his shoulder, the younger one thought the better of it. He dashed to catch up with the moving vehicle, and darted inside as the door swung open.

By this time, all roses by the street agreed. Something was amiss.

"Someone's gotta warn Master John," said the orange one. The yellow one nodded in the gravest deliberation.

"Yes, but how?" Another voice came, too soft for Artie to tell whose it was. "Let's not forget what the old codger reminded us. We are just plants."

Artie peered toward the part of the sky where the bright light had shown just moments before the human voices on the sidewalk spoke. The strong light was gone, and in its place was a string of stars that looked like they were not only smiling, but also winking at Artie. Artie suddenly remembered a tale of a human event long, long ago.

"Fire up the lights as bright as you can!" Artie shouted as loud as she could. It startled Blood-Red, right next to her.

"What good would that do?" Some roses asked.

"Just moved into the neighborhood and already giving orders," remarked others.

With a strength of character from Artie's lineage, she explained that a sudden surge of maximum power in the electrical lines might make the house's electric lines overload and short-circuit the electric lines. "What good would that do?" Blood-Red asked.

"At least, it'll get his attention!" JFK replied.

Without much experience in depending upon Master John for sustenance, Artie fought off her own apathy, and completed her thought, "Once we get his attention, we can alert him to the peril."

"OK, one thing at a time. We'll see if Artie's right," replied the orange rose.

The roses tried once more to get Chauncey's attention. He was their connection to the residence's electrical system.

Chauncey remarked, "I've been listening to you. I heard some things coming from people on the sidewalk. I don't know what all the ruckus is about. If I start a short-circuit, I'll just be in the trash can by tomorrow morning. It's bad enough that this is probably my last Christmas!"

Just then, the vehicle carrying the two lads swung around the corner and parked by the curb in front of the house. "Nothing like a couple of doughnuts and some hot coffee to give you some up and-at-'em," said the younger one through an open window. This even Chauncey heard.

The unmistakable metallic click of a firearm's triggering mechanism sounded ominously in the yard. Artie was the only rose in the garden not to recognize the sound.

Chauncey threw caution to the wind. He heard footsteps inside the house, reaching for the front door. It would only be seconds before the door swung open to Master John's danger.

Chauncey knew little about electronics. He knew even less about electrons, neutrons, and magnetic fields. He did know how to boost the joules in his circuitry, having seen a cantankerous old line of bulbs do it when he was first attached to the line. This was an opportunity to prove that he was not 'over-the-hill'.

Suddenly, surging the electrical current through his own and his neighbors' lines, Chauncey led the charge. The apolitical, seemingly inattentive lines fresh from the box and the keener, cognizant lines that had weathered many a storm all shone as brightly as they could. They reacted electrically, sending voltage coursing through the lines to the central circuit-breaker inside the garage. The house and the yard went dark.

"Honey," came the unmistakable voice of Master John, just inside the front door. "Where's the flash-light?"

"Same place it always is, dear," Mary answered. "Over by the lantern, just next to the refrigerator."

John's footsteps were heard, leaving the front door, hitting the linoleum in the kitchen. Chauncey became concerned. What if the only effect of this action was to hasten Chauncey's demise? He sent a silent message back down the electrical lines, that they could back off their surge. The objective seemed to have been accomplished.

Chapter 4
Intrusion

The two attackers seemed unperturbed by the sudden darkness of the exterior and the interior of the house. The brilliance of the stars had declined, but there was still enough light from the stars above, for them to make headway to the front door. One staked out the corner of the garage by the sidewalk leading to the door, while the other approached the front door, shotgun carried at the waist.

Chauncey tried to unravel from his attachment to the neighboring lines, but the prongs held him firmly. He cast forlorn glances of ineffective dismay at the roses, but none of them could help. They all looked downward, as though staring at the ground would motivate it to release them suddenly.

Bernie, dangling in the total darkness of the Christmas tree inside, had an inspiration. Other lights and ornaments on the tree had registered their disgust with the inconsistency of power burn-outs in the holiday season. Bernie had overheard the planning and realized that this one was intentional.

The light closest to him, a few branches away, had claimed that it served the Master right for all the months he made the electrical lines and ornaments wait in their boxes, until at last, in early December, they would finally be taken out, tested, cast aside, or hung up. Boxes of decorations that had been too fit to throw out but not cute enough to reach the tree sat in the corner, awaiting their ultimate demise.

Other decorations carried on the cacophony of disgust that, on this of all nights, the electricity would fail. Bernie wondered at their disloyalty. With only three options, hanging from a tree to mark a notable event in human history, one month out of twelve in the year, seemed rather an honor than a cruel fate.

When John found the flashlight and made his way to the door, Bernie could see from the reflection in the window pane of the grandfather clock that he was carrying pliers and screwdriver with the torch. He stopped momentarily to look out the peep hole of the front door, but muttered disgustedly as he remembered that the Christmas wreath on the door blocked the view through the hole.

He swung the door open with the flashlight shining forward from his hip. The light fell quickly on the young man with the shotgun at the doorstep.

"What do you want?" John asked the intruder.

"John, what is it?" Mary's voice came from inside.

"We want a little visit with you," said the armed man. Just then, his accomplice appeared, armed with a handgun and a knife in his belt.

"Well, you could have done that in reasonable hours," said John, ignoring the shotgun. The roses perked their heads up in the background, Chauncey tried to spark some glow back in his bulbs, and Bernie trained his ears keenly for more information.

John was actually not very surprised to see these home invaders. He had thought for several years, since the internet made contacts across the continent and from country to country more feasible, that someday his feared enemies would come for him, seeking revenge. He had played football in college and he left a trail of hatred in his wake, not just from his athletic achievements, but also from his adept self-defense.

Pars Duo

Chapter 5
The Cause

John was just a 128-pound cornerback playing for a college club football team, when his team was visited by Paterson State College, a team bent on making a name for itself. He had come into the game midway through the first quarter, when the visitors had already scored once, and were threatening again.

The first down was uneventful, but on the next snap, the Paterson State quarterback, apparently seeking to take advantage of an undersized second-stringer, had thrown to a 6'2" tight end being covered by John at his 20-yard line.

John had good position on the receiver, being between him and the goal line, but wanted to shake the ball loose from the taller offensive player. As the end left the ground in a half-leap to catch a slightly-overthrown pass, John reared his head back and slammed it into the receiver's groin area, just after the ball had arrived.

The ball came loose but the receiver was hung up on the back of John's helmet. Being of rather stout girth for a 128-pounder, John flicked his head to cause the opposition player to fall backward, off the back of his shoulders.

If John had been bigger, the movement might have seemed like a rodeo bull tossing a rider from the saddle.

John had been nonchalant about returning to the defensive huddle when the receiver came up on him from behind. Apparently, having been offended by the way in which the pass had been rendered incomplete, the receiver wanted to grab John and take him down, but John's teammates warned him of the on-coming assault and John saw him coming from the corner of his eye.

John ducked at the last minute and the end slid over his right shoulder. John took his right hand and wrapped it over the back of the end's helmet. He flipped him over his shoulder and continued his walk to the defensive huddle while the receiver landed on his upper back at the ground by his feet.

After the huddle broke, and John's teammates had their signals, John went to the other end of the field, and stood in wait for the receiver on that side to come out of the offensive huddle. Instead, John saw the same unhappy receiver approaching him at a half-gallop, slowing down as he reached John.

John took a step toward the receiver, and as his foot reached the ground on that step, the receiver raised a large fist and started to swing it in the direction of John's face.

John's brother had given him some tips on the basics of self-defense a few months before the season had started. John did not expect to use any of them because he thought it was just football, which is supposed to be a sport, after all. But John listened respectfully, remembering that his brother had left the sport when he had been beaten up after practice by one of his own teammates back in the Midwest.

John moved his arms and hands forward in a sweeping motion over his head, ducking the punch from the unhappy receiver simultaneously. Just after the intended blow swished the air above his head, John's own blow struck the receiver heavy, right above the point where the eyebrows met and the nose began.

The blow was a clean one, with maximum force, and it sent the receiver toppling backward in a heap. John knew that it had achieved maximum effectiveness.

John walked back toward the area where his defense had huddled. The offense had left their huddle, but stood just before the scrimmage line, watching what transpired between John and his adversary. After a moment of awkward silence, John said to the referee without turning his head, "You better get someone to pick him up. He's not getting up on his own."

Indeed, the young man was never to rise to his feet again. He was taken by cart from the field, and by ambulance to the hospital, where he had been determined 'dead on arrival'.

John assumed that the intrusion that Christmas Eve was related to that incident many years before. He had led a relatively quiet life, seldom gaining public attention, steadily from that incident.

Chapter 6
Back to the House

It turned out that the two intruders wanted to talk to John for a few minutes before getting on with their plan. They wanted to make sure they had the right guy, and they wanted to tease him a bit with the hope of evading his apparent fate. The younger one was too young to have been on the field the day that John earned their revenge, but the older one, once he stepped into the light, was in that range.

The conversation sped back to those days, with the gunmen's observation that there were no football trophies or other awards in the living room. Next came the taunt.

"I would at least have expected that you'd have some ribbons from karate competitions, judo tournaments, or tai kwan do bouts," the younger one said.

"I never fought professionally," John answered. By this time, the older one had him bound with his hands behind his back by duct tape. They kept his mouth free to engage in conversation.

John was reminded of some of the other events that happened that same day on the football field.

After the first attacker was taken off the field, others came at him, starting with those who tried to take him out when he was punting. It wasn't that difficult because of the porous line that was supposed to hold them off.

The first tore through the line before the long snap even reached John. He realized that the only way he was going to get the kick off was if he were to turn around, face the opposite direction, and snap the kick backward over his head. This cut the contact time between rusher and punter by three strides, the two normally taken toward the line of scrimmage, and the third consisting of the length of his leg as it whipped it backward.

His coach thought John was kicking it the wrong direction. He screamed, but by then John had put his foot into motion. The contact from the rusher came almost simultaneously with the ball leaving John's foot. Since John didn't know if the contact had occurred before the ball left his foot, he had to follow through with his kicking leg, in case the punt was not disallowed by the roughing penalty.

John snapped his leg back in time to avoid being pressed like a turkey's wishbone with his pelvis grinding into the ground. The ref threw the flag because the punt was gone long before the contact had been made. John got up and dusted himself off.

Later, John was in formation to punt much closer to the opponent's goal line. He received a low snap and again saw rushers pouring through his line to make a blocked punt a virtual assurance. He faked a motion like the beginning of a punt and then darted to his right. He realized that he could get past the first defenders on that side, but there were others closing in from the secondary, both in the center and on the far right.

He pulled up, realizing that the ground below him was just hard enough to sustain some bounce.

John dropped the ball and started his kicking motion. He had not tried a drop kick in several years but it came back to him quickly. The timing on the kick was the main difficulty. If he stroked the ball before it hit the ground, it would not be a legitimate drop kick. If he kicked it too late, it would go off to one side or another, but would not rise toward the goalposts.

The contact with the on-coming rusher this time happened squarely in his front. He was moving upward with the kicking motion when the rusher struck him full force, mostly on his left side. He was still moving upward as the rusher's momentum drove him backward. They were both off the ground at this time.

John twisted enough to his right and then turned back toward his left, so that he could release from the contact by the opponent. Luckily, the offender had not grabbed onto him. John realized that his back was turning backward, making a landing at that angle risky. He knew that his shoulders were going to hit the ground first.

He rolled more back toward his right and decided that a landing on that side would break his collarbone. He swiveled quickly back toward his left, causing his left upper back to take the brunt of the impact. The rest of his body fell in a heap.

John took mental inventory of himself and decided that he was healthy enough to try to get up. As he rose to his feet, the crowd let loose a roar. The kick had sailed through the uprights, making for a field goal.

The ref had thrown a flag for roughing the punter.

The captain called John over to take part in the decision about accepting or declining the penalty. John gave a hands-over-head 'OK' signal to his coaches and turned to tell Captain Bobby, "I want those 3 points."

Some in the crowd breathed a sigh of relief. Others expressed indignation that the penalty was declined. They wanted the first down and an opportunity to score a touchdown. But, on the kickoff, John drove the ball hard into a lineman at the front of the opposing team, and sent it sailing high above that player's head.

As he waited for it to come down, John narrowed in on him and timed his block just so that it would hit shortly after the ball had gone through the lineman's arms. He left it to his teammate to recover the fumble and leveled the lineman. When he looked up, the ball was in his teammate's hands and they had it back, a few dozen yards back from where they would have had it if they had declined the penalty.

Another time that same day, John received a slow snap for a punt, and started his motion deliberately and normally, as if the defensive lineman were not bearing down on him. He pulled the ball back in as the lineman made contact on his right side, anticipating that the kick would come from that side.

Instead, as he fell, John reached out with his left hand and, holding the ball on that side, got a punt off while falling to the ground. He realized that none of his teammates would know that he had gotten the punt away. He had been watching the referee from the corner of his left eye, to stop the play if the ref blew the whistle before he kicked the ball.

John hustled down to the 5-yard line and downed the punt before anyone else on the field could react. Some in the crowd apparently thought that he could recover possession, as if it had been an on-sides kick, but their neighbors explained when John just touched the ball and kept running past it.

There was also a play when John was supposed to punt but he realized that the on-coming rusher would block it if he didn't do something about it.

He started his punting motion normally but let the ball squirt off the right side of his foot, carrying downfield enough to be outside the reach of the punt returned who was situated directly downfield from the scrimmage line.

While his punting leg was in the air, the defender made contact with him at the lower torso, carrying his weight directly backward.

John used is left foot to catch the defender between his legs and twist his head toward the side. He then leveled his own position out to descend about evenly with the defender.

As they approached the ground, John pulled his legs downward, as if to knock the defender out with the impact with the ground. Realizing that he might cause more damage to his leg than he wanted, John pulled up with the legs and made a soft impact with the defender's head, to cause him to concuss but not to damage his own legs.

Chapter 7
Confrontation

John snapped back to attention to the two men threatening his life in his living room several years later. He thought to himself, *"Funny how the mention of kung fu can take your mind back to the wrong things."* There had been no martial arts involved with the punts, but if he had not known how to take a fall, a fundamental element of karate, he would never have finished the game that day.

Then again, John thought, it could have been one of four other events that day long ago.

He was playing defensive secondary on the right side when a receiver cut from the center in his direction, passing before him about 5 yards up-field. John stood his ground and thought this would be too easy. However, the throw was almost out of reach, leading him too far in the direction of the right sideline. The receiver dove for it; John was content to let it fall incomplete.

Instead, the receiver put his hands on it and seemed about to land on the ground with a phenomenal catch. John moved to his right and stood about at the receiver's waist as he gathered in the ball. John told him in a calm voice, "Drop the ball, kid."

The receiver yelled something negative and grasped the ball tighter. After John hit the receiver just above the waist with both arms locked together in a volleyball's digger position, he said "Please drop the ball." The receiver prepared himself for some contact but maintained a tight grip on the ball.

John moved around toward the receiver's legs and hit him again while he was still suspended in mid-air, this time using the same type of blow but mid-thigh, between the knees and waist. Finally, John said, "Last chance, kid, drop the ball."

The receiver again yelled something confrontational; now John had moved up by his head. He unloaded with his forearms just above the receiver's chinstrap, sending him flipping backward and hitting his head hard against the ground.

The receiver lost consciousness immediately and John leaned over to pick up the ball. Concerned about the receiver, John took a knee and leaned in to see if he was alright.

The receiver's teammate brushed John off. John left the ball on the ground and headed for the sideline, signaling change of possession as he did.

The referee had signaled a completion when the receiver first grasped the ball and brushed the ground with his right foot. Once the ball was loose, he had to call it a fumble.

In another play, the coach had inserted him into the line-up as safety. It was fourth down and the opposing team was at the 20-yard line. They needed 10 full yards for a first down.

John thought it would be ridiculous for them to settle for 10 yards when, for double the distance, they could have a touchdown. He lined up at the 5-yard line, ready to make the stop if the pass was thrown for the 10-yard gain, but more anticipating the catch was to be attempted at the goal line.

The pass came as the receiver ran directly toward John. The ball was again overthrown and again the receiver dove for it. John timed his own dive for the contact helmet-to-helmet with the receiver just after the ball arrived.

The ball was never taken into control. The receiver was slow rising. John strode toward the other sideline, taunting the coach by yelling, "Nice call, Coach! Not too obvious or anything!"

The third play was also near his team's goal line. John moved in from the cornerback position to help the end seal off a run. He landed on his knees to block the runner's advance after the initial contact with the end.

As the runner fell down, a blocker for the runner fell across John's lower legs. John thought it looked contrived, so he looked behind him to see another player from the opposing team begin a short sprint in his direction.

Realizing that his legs were pinned down so he couldn't get up, and seeing the player running his direction, John leaned forward to make it harder for the player to judge when to dive in his direction. Then, as the player slowed down to adjust his dive in the correct direction, John leaned back to confuse him more.

The player slowed down further, then dove toward John. John moved forward one, then twice more, and then pushed his back toward the player as hard as he could, simulating a hard pop with his back.

The contact hit the player solidly at the top of the helmet just after he had taken off. With nothing to brace against to absorb the shock, the player took the impact and vibration through the helmet to his head. He fell unconscious to the ground.

John was afraid he might have been more seriously injured than others imagined. He crawled his direction and checked him. The eyes were shut and the breathing was shallow.

John lifted his helmet off and began giving the player mouth-to-mouth resuscitation. Some smart-alec in the crowd yelled, "The kiss of death."

John tried for moments to bring the player around, but he was not reviving. John realized that he was probably exhaling carbon dioxide into the player's lungs, instead of oxygen. He felt the player's pulse and looked at his purple fingernails. Then he went to work feverishly, alternately pushing the player's stomach down and puffing wind into his lungs, finally reviving him with light slaps to the face.

Even before the player opened his eyes, the player yelled, "I hate Catholics!"

John told him, "Shut up, kid." The guy yelled it again; John told him, "Kid, you're at Catholic University, shut up!"

Then the kid yelled it again. John's response was to punch the player in the mouth, sending blood and bone of his teeth running all directions.

John left the player on the ground and started toward his own sideline, taking his helmet completely off. His coaches waved him back to the game.

John thought he would be kicked out of the game, even though it wasn't his fault. He had hit another player, but the referees said nothing about it.

As the player was being led off the field, John yelled toward him, "Try it again, punk. I'll kill you next time."

Then, earlier in the game, John had been lying on his back after having made a difficult tackle. He thought about getting up right away, but he hesitated. It was good that he did not get up immediately.

A player from the other team came flying across from downfield and buried his helmet into John's chest. John exaggerated the pain to make sure that the referee called the penalty.

The referee called the penalty for unsportsmanlike conduct on the opposing player. While he was marking off the yardage, John took careful note of the player's number—55.

Later in the game, John was in position to break up a short pass to a receiver. He was set to jump up with the receiver when a voice from the crowd yelled, "John, it's number 55."

John looked at the receiver's jersey and saw the number 55. Instead of going up with him to compete for the pass, John waited until the receiver had caught it and started his descent toward the earth.

John lunged upward and extended his forearms in a double-shiver movement. The forearms caught the receiver below the jaw and his head jerked backward.

The receiver dropped the ball and John turned sideways to begin a karate chop toward the receiver's nose. His coach called from the sideline, "John, don't do it."

John let the receiver go, but as he fell to the ground, the receiver swung one arm weakly toward him. John's hands were above his head to assure that the ref didn't think he was taking advantage of the receiver's vulnerable position to hit him again.

The referee threw the flag for a personal foul on the receiver. John walked nonchalantly to the huddle as the receiver slumped to the ground.

Pars Tres

Chapter 8
The Comeback

John heard Mary's voice from the back room.

"Who is it, John?" The invaders realized there was someone else in the house. Before she could get a call off to 911, they had seized her and dragged her out to the front room where John was already tied up.

While they were tying Mary up, John's mind returned to the day when this all started. Instinctively, he began to taunt the invaders. He reminded them that his team had actually taken the lead when late in the game, he marched them downfield with a series of short passes to the tight ends, one on each side.

John's mind turned to the details while the intruders discussed what they were going to do with Mary. Eventually, the leader said that they would leave her there. "Our quarrel isn't with her," he said.

Before he had gone out to resume possession, his coach extracted a promise from him, that he would keep the ball on the ground, and just hand it off. Presumably, he wanted to run the clock down before taking the lead.

John had already made up his mind to try the short passes to tight ends, to go without a huddle in-between plays, and to hold the ball as long as he could before he attempted each pass.

The last of these proved to be nearly disastrous.

John's front line was porous in that it let the defenders through as if by design.

John realized that they were near the goal line, but it would take more than two seconds from the snap of the ball, for the receivers to get into position to score a touchdown. One and a half seconds from snap, he yelled, "Right," and the receivers looked over their right shoulders.

Unfortunately, the defenders were keying on this tactic and both shifted one-half man's distance to their left, to overplay that side of each receiver. A half-beat later, John shifted the ball to his left hand and began his throwing motion as if to arc the pass high over the receivers' heads downfield.

John then pulled the ball down and made a jerking motion as if to try to juke the defender out of position and run past him. The defender pulled his arms down to push directly toward John, rather than to block what had seemed to be a high pass delivery.

John took this instant to level a hard pass on the line directly off the defender's right shoulder, toward the receiver's left side. The defender accelerated into John but it was too late to have an effect on the pass. The ball was already on its way.

Just before John hit the ground, he shouted, "No, left!" The receiver made the adjustment to the ball and caught for the score easily.

John didn't see the connection until reviewing tapes after the game. His elbows were pinned to the ground as the back of his helmet smacked against the ground.

The crowd roared its approval, and rising to his feet shakily, John gave the signal to his coaches that he was good for two more plays.

This come-back had begun with three touchdown passes in succession, when John was inserted into the lineup as third-string back-up quarterback. He had realized quickly that the rush from the defensive line was too strong for his blockers; he ran outside tackle and waited before crossing the scrimmage line.

As a defender was approaching him the first time, he surprised him by driving his helmet forward, initiating the contact with the defender's helmet, and releasing the ball to Johnson with a step lead on his defender.

The second time, the same approach unfolded, but this time the rushing defender was not surprised by the sudden impact from John's helmet; nevertheless, when he drove through the contact, he did not drive John to the ground as forcefully as possible.

The third time the rushing defender did not let up, and drove John as hard to the ground as he could. Like the other two passes, Johnson grabbed them and took them to pay dirt, oblivious to the collision between quarterback and rusher.

This time, John kept his face in the ground, trying to think of a reason why he should get up. He saw the crowd roaring happily from the corner of his eye, and thought,

"Why should I get up? I've already done more for this school today than all those others sitting in the grand-stands."

Before he had a chance to answer his own question, one of his teammates came over, offered his hand to help John up, and lifted him up when John complied. John resolved that he would not need a teammate's assistance on anything for the rest of the day.

Chapter 9
Gathering Momentum

The next opportunity came as John was running the same roll-out to the right, but this time Johnson was covered completely. He looked for his secondary receiver, who has stopped at the 10-yard line, trying to guess where John was going with the ball. John gave him a palms-up gesture, telling him effectively to choose his route.

With the urgency shown in his face, John communicated that something needed to be done quickly. The receiver started slowly down the left sideline toward the goal, and John realized that, with the distance the ball would have to travel to reach the receiver, he would have to lead him about half-way through the end zone to make a completion.

John bent his back and let the ball fly. The receiver quickened his pace and gathered in the pass with room to spare in the end-zone. Suddenly, the Paterson State team and its coach realized they were in a game for real.

Playing off this sequence, on their next possession, John took Freddie, a lineman, with him to the far right and set up behind him, with the receiver running the same routes. He pumped the ball toward the left but did not release.

He sidestepped to his left and faked a throwing motion to Johnson who was now double-covered. Ass all his receivers were over twenty yards downfield, he handed the ball to his lineman to carry by tucking it under his right elbow, and telling him, "Go!"

Freddie made good yardage, as the defenders downfield did not realize it was a running play, until he had almost come up behind them.

Freddie next came in handy on the same formation with a roll-out to the left. This time, he set up behind John near the left sideline, and John looked undecided on where to go with the ball.

John faked a screen pass to a short receiver just over the line of scrimmage. He made a jerky motion as if he were thinking of tucking the ball and running with it himself.

John knew that the defensive line expected him to hand the ball off cleverly to Freddie again. As they started to close in on him, he called out to Freddie, "Now!"

Freddie stepped up and took on the rushing defensive lineman with a straight-up block that stood him up in his tracks. John used the moment's opening to throw the ball back across to Johnson, who had made his way into the end zone on the right side.

It was an easy connection, and John's team clearly had the momentum now. There were still many points to make up.

Once when John thought that his half-back's dive over tackle would yield a touchdown, he started toward the sideline in anticipation of a break before the attempted point-after.

He looked up in alarm when he saw a defensive lineman running with the ball in the opposite direction. He shouted, "What happened?"

His helmet slipped off his head as he had already loosened the chinstrap.

There was an opposing player right behind John. He had to sidestep that player to avoid a block, and doing so cost him some more yardage in the chase to catch the opponent taking the fumble back for a touchdown. By the time he had done so, he was about 25 yards behind him and about 20 yards across the field.

John lengthened his stride and took heart from the fact that the ball-carrier was an overweight lineman. He made ground on him steadily, but the lineman was holding up with his strides. By this time, John was covering about 5 yards per step.

As they reached the 10-yard line, John realized that, to catch the opponent, he would have to jump the last few steps. He took leaps rather than running strides and barely caught the opponent, pushing him out of bounds at about the 2-yard line.

When John got up, he wanted to be assured that he could be in on the goal line stand to prevent the touchdown he had avoided by running the distance of the field. He motioned for his teammates to take his helmet out to him from where it lay on the ground over 80 yards away.

They did so, and one of them tossed it to him from about 15 feet away, when they huddled up for defense.

John waited until he heard the defensive signals before putting the helmet on. The first play was an attempted leap over the right offensive side; John had to run from his position as cornerback on the other side of the field, to leap himself just in time to collide head-to-head with the ball carrier, bringing him down for no gain.

On the second down, John was blocked effectively, but doing so opened up enough of a gap that one of his teammates beat his blocker and penetrated enough to stop the carrier from making any ground. John congratulated the teammate heartily when he returned to the huddle.

The next play was an incomplete pass.

John saw his chance to end their offense on the next play. Paterson State lined up for a field goal. John took his usual place to the right, to try to get in to block the kick. When Paterson State came out of the huddle, a large player was positioned directly opposite him.

John waited until the signal-caller began to set the line before him. After 'Down! Set', John quickly shifted to his left just enough to get a break between the blocker assigned to him and the end on that side. John lowered his head and waited for the snap.

John got a good break on the ball. As it was snapped, he got across with enough speed to enable his lateral leap to stand a chance for him to get his hands on the ball.

As the kicker stepped toward the ball, John extended as far as he could. He reached out with his fingers, and the tips touched the ball as it released from the kick without rotating.

John pushed the ball to the side, pulled his right leg up beneath him, used it to jettison himself up field, and maintained enough balance to be there when the Paterson State player picked up the ball before it went out of bounds.

When John lightly tossed him onto his side, possession of the ball was going over to John's team at the 15-yard line.

On another field goal attempted later by Paterson State, John cruised through from right cornerback into what he considered an open gap between blockers, to get a clean shot at the block.

He was surprised by a blocker who lunged from his right to knock him down short of the tee. John was further surprised when he looked up to see that he was a short arm's length away from the ball.

Just as he reached out to knock the ball off the tee, the foot came through from the kicker. John barely pushed the ball off to the side, onto the ground, before the foot slammed into the side of his helmet.

John was grateful that he did not raise his head any higher than he did. The kicker's foot would have struck him directly in the eye. As it was, the Paterson State possession was halted harmlessly.

John's first blocked field goal, however, was a more standard type. He illegally used his teammate's back to gain extra altitude on a jump after the hike was made. He rose as high as he could.

When the ball struck his hands, he did not try to bat the ball away. Instead, he held onto it and let the ball give slightly as he did so, keeping it in his grasp. He was tackled shortly afterward.

Pars Quattro

Chapter 10
Incendiary Tactics

By this time, with Mary secured in the back of the house with duct tape on her mouth and her arms bound, John tried to return to the present, but his mind kept returning to the events that led to this intrusion.

John remembered keeping the pace up with a series of runs that developed as power sweeps right, then pitch-outs left, back and forth, without a huddle, gathering yardage as the march continued.

When the defense started realizing that the next play was going to the side opposite of the last play, they started stacking the line on that side, and John needed to leave his post as quarterback to get an extra block in, to gain yardage instead of being stopped for a loss.

Then, when the defense expected a run right, John took the snap, made a step in that direction, swiveled and pivoted 270 degrees to put the ball on his left side, and began a run directly up the left.

There were defenders on that side, but the offensive players he had set up to take the ball that direction on the previous play provided adequate blocking for him to twist and turn his way into the end zone.

Things became ugly when John was playing defense. He broke up plays that came his way indiscriminately. In gestures, John told the opposing quarterback, "Keep on throwing into my territory! You'll have all your receivers on crutches!"

This did not win him a lot of admirers on the Paterson State team.

Once John looked up from his defensive coverage just in time to see an opposing player squatting over his best receiver. Johnson was pinned with his back to the ground. He heard a voice yell, "John, help him!"

John waited until he saw the opposing player's right fist start to lower toward Johnson. He took a step and lunged toward the offender, driving his helmet into his spine, moving him off Johnson. Then as he gathered himself up from spreading out the aggressor on the ground, he put his foot on the guy's neck and grabbed his facemask.

In the manner of a Roman gladiator giving the crowd or the emperor the right to call the next move, he motioned toward the Paterson State coach, asking him, "Thumbs up or Thumbs down?"

The surprised Paterson State player squirmed to get out from under the pressure of John's cleat, but John just pushed harder against his neck, nearly crushing his windpipe. The player stopped squirming to await his fate rather than hasten it.

When John received no response from the Paterson State coach at first, he again emphasized his gesture, clearing giving the coach the choice of whether he would deliver the coup de grace.

This time, the coach signaled 'Thumbs up', and walked away from his place on the sideline. John let the player go and he scrambled to his feet to get away from the psychotic.

Things deteriorated between the Paterson State team and John. Between plays, when John was playing cornerback on the right side, just a few yards from the visitors' bench, he yelled for the Paterson State coach.

When the coach looked at him, John used his left hand to cover the indecent gesture he was making with his right hand, so that he wouldn't draw a penalty from one of the referees. The coach was incensed but there was nothing anyone could do about it, since no ref saw it.

Still later in the game, John looked up to see another Paterson State player squatting over Bobby, another teammate. This time, he did not wait until the arm started down toward his teammate before making a move.

John lunged forward and grabbed the offender under the armpits. His momentum carried him past the two on the ground. As he was about to lose grip on the Paterson State player, he swung his hips backward and picked the player up off the ground.

John swung the opposing player around behind him and threw him like a javelin a good 10 yards away from his teammate.

Then, to guarantee that the player would not come back again, John walked in his direction with his hands clenched in fists and carried a little above his waistline.

The player obstinately scampered to his feet and rushed past John, in the direction of Bobby. John tackled him from behind, and pushed his shoulders over. He lowered his face toward the player and said, "You either respect us or you crawl from this field. Make your mind up quick."

The player replied, "Respect." John let him up. He scrambled off, this time in the direction of the Paterson State bench.

Chapter 11
Deception

More reminiscing while the intruders carried him off took John to his telepathy with Johnson. Their coach sent in a fast halfback to aid in their next offensive series. Johnson called a play in which the halfback would run to his left, all others would set up a blocking wall before him, and the play would run around that side.

As they set up at the line of scrimmage, John noticed that the defense seemed to anticipate a running play, with most of their formation close to the line of scrimmage. This left single coverage on Johnson to the far right.

John made the calls to the center, who hiked the ball. John pivoted to his right as planned. The halfback and his blocking wall took off to the left. John began the pitch-out motion but did not release the ball.

No one was approaching John. They all seemed to expect him to send the play around to the left.

When John turned back to face the scrimmage line, still no defender came his direction. Johnson was still at the line of scrimmage on the right side. John tucked the ball and began a lurch toward the scrimmage line, but stayed where he had taken the hike.

Now it was decision time. His team would lose whatever element of surprise they might have if he did not start a play one direction or the other. He clearly was not running the ball.

He lofted a pass that drifted slowly about 10 yards up the right sideline, within reach of Johnson if he started moving. Still there came no move by Johnson. John's shoulders slumped, as he was just about resigned to having thrown his first incompletion of the day.

Suddenly, Johnson made a double-fake move and broke up the sideline as if struck from behind by lightning. When John saw Johnson's hands close on the ball, he let out a cheer and pumped his fist in the direction of the visitors' bench.

There was no catching Johnson from behind on that play. Nothing stopped him until he reached the goal line.

John avoided the looks from his teammates as they undoubtedly felt duped by John's change in the play called in the huddle.

Chapter 12
Post-Game Interviews

Finally, John realized how his celebrity had induced his intruders to go after him even years after these events. Meanwhile, Mary was trying to find the keys to her car.

After the game, John was approached by national media. The first reached him before he had made it off the field. The interviewer wanted to know his opinion of a play in which he had avoided personal injury, but had scored the first three points on a drop kick.

John replied that this particular player had gone beyond trying to block the kick, and wanted to ram him into the ground at an awkward, mid-air position. "There are some players who lose sight of the object of the game. They get so focused on intimidating the other team that they forget about playing it fundamentally and fairly," he said.

The interviewer wanted a more direct response.

John tried again, "Some players think more about injuring players on the other team than they do about winning the game. This guy was clearly out to injure me. He didn't care if he gave up some points or a first down doing so."

Still the interviewer persisted. John's response was, "I think this guy's sick."

When the interviewer still didn't seem to get the point, John added, "I think you're sick," and trotted off.

Before he reached the top of the stairs to the locker room, another sportscaster, introducing himself at Dick Stockton, approached with a cameraman, ready to ask him for comments.

John indicated that he was familiar with the man, saying, "I've admired your work."

Stockton asked John for his comments on the game. John addressed 'the kids out there'. He told them to, "get your homework done first, before going out to play sports after school. The books will take you a lot farther in life than some ball will."

Stockton gave him a chance for another comment. John addressed youngsters thinking of playing quarterback in the future. "Kids who want to play quarterback, it's not enough to put a spiral on the ball. If you don't tilt the nose of the ball up as it spins on the axis, it will arc too much, the ball can drift and some defensive back can come across and pick it off, like a cherry off a tree."

Stockton understood and said, "Just as you did a few times over there."

The sportscaster asked for another comment. John said, "You guys out there who want to make interceptions when you get your hands on the ball, don't push your hands out on contact. Give way a bit with the ball so it doesn't bounce off your hands and hit the ground."

"Soft hands," Stockton said.

One last chance for a comment was given. John was disconcerted about making spur-of-the moment public comments so he made his last statement political.

"Get your asses out of Vietnam," he snorted, and jogged up the aisle toward the locker room without waiting for another question.

Pars Cinco

Chapter 13
Left-Sideline Receptions

A few miles down the road, the intruders stopped the car on a side-road and pulled John out. They started beating him, first with their fists and later with sticks or poles.

John lost consciousness and went into a reverie, dimly recalling his time as a receiver that crucial day.

The defense was doing its part, but also some Paterson State scores came too quickly to afford his offensive squad much time off the field. Some catches he made up the left sidelines would have made for a full day themselves:

The most remarkable came on a throw that John judged to be too high for him to reach. He was in the corner of the end zone, and no defender was near him. As he jumped as high as he could, he thought to himself, *"At least no one will blame me for not having tried."*

To his surprise, the ball settled into his outstretched hands. He clasped it firmly and then twisted slightly to his left to show the referee that he had control of it. He knew this wouldn't be enough for a reception.

John thought, *"Here comes the hard part."* He did not try to cushion his fall with an elbow or with one arm outstretched. He knew that the impact with the ground would shake the ball loose if he tried that tactic.

John held the ball with both hands above the crest of his head, and stretched his feet out behind him to get them in the end zone to make a completion for a score. As he landed flat face down on the ground, his face mask provided some cushion as his face flopped downward. He felt that he would have lost consciousness if it were not for the face mask.

As he gathered his composure, lying face down on the ground, he lifted the ball up with his right hand and waved it slightly behind his helmet. Once he heard the crowd roar, he realized that the ref must have signaled a catch.

John let the ball drop behind his helmet and put his hands on the ground. He paused a moment before pushing himself off the ground and making his way to the huddle. He did not acknowledge cheers from the crowd.

On another play, John was being covered closely by a cornerback as he released from the left split end position. He ran a route at about a 45-degree angle toward the sideline. The defender was cutting of the area on his left shoulder, but he knew that was where his quarterback would throw it.

To avoid giving the cornerback an even chance to reach the ball, John looked back over his right shoulder. This convinced the cornerback not to look up for the ball, but rather to focus on trying to close the space between John's right shoulder and the place where he thought the trajectory would lead the ball to descend.

Then, estimating when the ball would arrive on his left, John ended the decoy and looked back to that side. Seeing the ball come in, John reached up and drew it in before the cornerback could make an adjustment and deflect the ball.

John had managed to get his feet in-bounds before reaching the sideline. After the ref blew the whistle, both players returned to their huddles exchanging compliments. "Nice catch," said the cornerback.

"Nice cover," said John.

On another catch at the sideline, John realized that he was going too fast to get a foot down before going out of bounds. He did a half-jump and flipped his legs over his head, coming down with his feet in a somersault that enabled him to bring them down in-bounds.

The closest defender was too surprised to do anything but watch him.

On another play, John realized that the defender behind him would not be satisfied with pushing him out of bounds, after he made the catch. With his feet still in the air, holding onto the ball, John began the usual motion to bring them down just below them.

Then he lifted them up quickly, only to see that the defender had crashed his helmet into the ground, right about where his feet would have been had it touched down normally.

The defender had tried to crush John's ankles on the play. John instead spread his feet out wide enough to get them down on either side of the defender, still in bounds, as the defender winced at having made contact with hard earth alone.

To add to his repertoire, John realized once playing cornerback that he was too far out of bounds in the air to complete a catch with his feet touching down in-bounds.

John twisted 180 degrees around and tapped the ball backward to Johnson who was playing safety about 7 yards inside the sideline. His teammate gathered it in and made a nice gain a few yards up-field to avoid the incompletion.

When the same play developed later in the game, John realized that this time the opposition was covering his teammates who would have received a tap-in from his awkward, out of bounds position. John pulled the pass in while hanging in mid-air, made a 90-degree twist to face up-field, and passed the ball to his teammate with his left hand.

Having completed a short forward pass to a teammate, he understood why the ref threw the flag (illegal forward pass).

However, the referees conferred and the call was overruled, with the explanation that, since John had not set down on the ground before passing, it could not be considered a forward pass. It had to be considered a tip from one teammate to another. The play was allowed.

Chapter 14
Conventional Field Goal-Kicking

John was returning to consciousness when his captors dragged him back into the car. He thought he remembered being afforded the opportunity to do some conventional placekicking that day.

Once when the offense stalled about the 40-yard line, their coach yelled to him, "John, can you make a field goal from there?"

"I never tried," was his response.

The coach said, "Well, try it now!"

John lined up and licked his left hand from wrist to fingertips. He put the left arm in the air to judge the strength of the wind. It was windy and the wind was blowing in his face. The snap came and John waited for the wind to die down. At first, the Paterson State players did not try to rush him, as they expected the attempt to come quickly, and the wind to bat it down.

But when they realized that he was waiting for the wind to die down, they started their rush. John got the kick off just in time, and watched it gain altitude as the wind had stopped briefly.

As the ball settled through the goalposts, John stood back in stunned amazement. His teammates rushed him as if he had kicked the game-winner. He just staggered backward as he realized that he had made a 52-yard field goal.

Later in the game, John was too obsessed with scoring a touchdown to line up and attempt a field goal on fourth down. When the snap came, he started forward as Freddie put the ball on the tee for him to kick. Instead of kicking it, however, he stumbled forward and pulled the ball up, gathering it in his forearms, and then taking it in his right hand.

Freddie yelled, "Fire," to let his teammates know that the field goal was not going to be attempted. John saw two defenders on the right side of the lines colliding at the scrimmage line. He had to out-maneuver them to get to the goal line.

John put his knees together and seemed designed on cutting inside the far defender, but almost directly at the close defender. He churned toward the scrimmage line. They were not taken off-guard.

John made contact with the close defender first, extending his left hand and catching him on the top of the helmet with a stiff-arm. Then he adjusted his knees inward, as if he would try to cut between him and the linemen still bunched up in the middle. The outer defender made a lunge in his direction, falling below John's still arm of the inner defender, as John pulled his legs away from both and more toward the sideline.

Now he had only the first defender to beat with his hand still on his helmet.

John had just about reached the line of scrimmage when he picked up the referee peering in from his right. He feared that the ref would call him for pushing the defender, if he kept the stiff-arm up as he cut toward the goal line. On the other hand, he needed it to prevent the defender from tackling him before he made it into the end zone.

John straightened his elbow but did not use his hand other than the palm to keep the defender in line. He accelerated as he best could, and let his arm drop as he gained the angle that would let him in for a score. The ref saw that he had not pushed the defender and blew the whistle for a touchdown when John crossed the goal line.

Chapter 15
The Show-Off

Mary gathered Miles and Sasha into her car. She drove off to reach John in the direction the GPS showed her.

Meanwhile, John remembered that, at least at one point, when he realized that the opposition's hand-offs and runs up the middle were gaining too much yardage, he had signaled for his coach to take him out.

When he reached the sideline, he flew behind the bench and crouched. He set up in a three-point stance and lurched forward first to bang the bench with the backs of his forearms and then to touch the bottom of the bench with his palms.

Then, he approached the defensive coordinator and asked him to put him in at defensive left guard for three plays. The coordinator did so reluctantly, knowing that John weighed much less than the offensive linemen he would be facing.

John reached the huddle and the teammate who had entered the game to replace him just a few moments earlier groaned, thinking that he was back to send him to the sidelines. John told the left guard he was in for him and the cornerback was allowed to stay.

Sure enough, the next play was a run up the middle. John ignored the runner and, on the snap, immediately stepped across the center, and released a double forearm-shiver on the offensive left guard. He used all the strength he could muster. His teammates made the tackle on the runner.

John watched his target make the return unsteadily to his huddle. A few moments later, that quarterback was asking for a substitution for that player, and he was helped to the sideline without needing a timeout. The next play was a hand-off and run directly at John.

John stepped once to his right to give the offensive linemen the notion that he would try to catch the runner from the side. Then as the linemen advanced, John dropped to his knees and clogged up the gap that would have let the runner through. He was stopped for no gain.

After the first defensive play, John had raised his left arm with two fingers extended, to show that he was only good for two more plays at that position. After this play, John again raised his left arm with a single digit extended, to show he meant to come out after the next play.

John shifted his feet as the offensive line came to the line. The center gave him a glance, as if to warn him they were coming his way. John made ready to submarine the next runner.

John was ready for a double-team but he expected it from linemen. Instead, one of the other running backs made his way behind the lead blocker to make it difficult for John to maintain his balance.

John chose to catch the first blocker by his shoulders and push him upright, so that the second blocker and the runner would have nowhere to go. Then, with all his might, he pushed and tried to send the first blocker backward into the second blocker.

This created enough interference for the defensive line to collapse on the runner, forcing a fourth down.

John was relieved when the coach sent the defensive lineman in to replace him.

Lucifer nodded approvingly, as if John was digging his own trench deeper.

John mentioned a later defensive play, when noticed that the quarterback was watching him, as he drifted back to make a pass. John drew some separation from the receiver he was defending, and taunted the quarterback by pointing in the direction of the receiver who was then unguarded.

The quarterback looked in that direction, and finally wound up to make the throw. At the same time, John started off to cover the ground that he had let grow between them. The quarterback's pass was slow and deliberate.

John picked up ground on the pass, but for a while it looked as if the only way he could prevent a reception would be to collide with the receiver simultaneously with the arrival of the ball. He covered the last 25 yards before the ball neared the receiver, and dove head-first toward the point where the ball was apparently going to land.

The receiver saw him coming and backed off enough for John to get his hands on the ball uninhibited by a competitor. He smacked the ball into the ground, and let his arms fall behind him, landing with his chest and his face simultaneously afterwards.

When he looked to the sideline, John's coach was not amused. John made an apologetic gesture and went back to the defensive huddle.

Later, when John was covering a receiver on the offense's right side of the field, he saw the same type of throw made toward a receiver being covered by Johnson on the left side.

John left his receiver and ran across on the frontside of the receiver, arriving just in time to pick the throw off with a one-handed leap over his head. John pulled the ball in, yelled, "Bingo" (as his coach had insisted the defensive backs were to exclaim on interceptions), and took the ball for about a 10-yard return before being tackled.

John got cleverer later in the game, when he saw that the quarterback was staring down the receiver he was covering in the middle of the field.

John knew he wouldn't throw if he stayed where he was, so he ran on the quarterback side of him, making it look like he was anticipating a throw at that moment. When the throw did not come, John threw his hands into the air as if exasperated that he had overplayed a potential interception.

John twisted backward around the receiver, to give the quarterback an open lane in which to throw to the receiver. Then, as the quarterback was unloading the pass, John rushed back around to the front of the receiver, making the play just as the ball arrived.

Another interception made John one of the opposition's most disfavored defenders that day.

On another play, John was watching the pass receivers who were coming off the offense's right side. One of them struck him in the lower jaw and attempted to grab him by the hands.

John slipped the grasp and noticed a running back releasing out of the backfield, just about 10 yards behind the receivers he was covering. He ducked around the receivers and reached the running back just as he was catching a short pass from the quarterback.

The play went for no gain; if he had stayed to mix it up with the receivers, the play would have gone for at least 10 yards.

The same type of play developed on the offense's left side later in the game. However, this time the running back in the flat was not the intended receiver.

When John released from the receiver who had tried to entice him into an altercation near the sideline, he saw another receiver farther downfield toward the middle. He abruptly left the receiver he had been covering, and was able to beat the mid-field receiver by twisting backward as he jumped about half-way up.

John held onto the ball as the intended receiver pulled him down for a tackle.

To top it off, when John was guarding an end who had just released from the scrimmage line, he kept a distance to encourage the quarterback to throw the ball. Then, he moved up closer to the end when he saw that the quarterback had thrown the ball.

The end knew that the ball was in the air but chose to watch John, in order to determine how to reach up to deflect it from him. John knew that it was coming in toward his left shoulder, but put his hands toward his right side to lure the end into staying out of the way of the ball's trajectory.

At the same time, the quarterback sensed that his throw was in trouble. He ran back toward the sideline to John's right, to protect against a potential post-interception run-back.

John switched his hands to the left just in time to catch the ball. The end looked surprised that he had not prevented the interception. Feeling cocky, John ignored the quarterback who was rushing to his side of the field, and stood a short distance from the receiver.

John held the ball out in the receiver's direction, as if to hand it to him. The receiver naively reached out to accept it from John, but John pivoted 300 degrees toward his left, coming out facing the goal line.

By then, the quarterback had closed much of the distance, and was only 5 to 10 yards away.

John ran as fast as he could up the sideline, chuckling to himself about the deception of the end. The quarterback lurched forward and swung his left arm with his fist clenched, to catch John across the helmet.

The contact sent John sprawling in a backward flip, with the ball popping out of his arm harmlessly out of bounds. John landed on his knees and ankles, laughing loudly by this time.

The ref, however, did not consider it funny. He threw a flag against the quarterback for a personal foul, blow to the head.

Pars Ses

Chapter 16
Offensive Receiver

Realizing that his plight might be becoming tenuous, John brought up the time, with the game nearing the end, John ran downfield on offense from the split end position. He faked around the defender and streamed down the sideline as fast as he could. He saw the ball leave the quarterback's hand, in his direction, but knew that he had led him too much.

John continued to gallop downfield, barely paying attention to the ball. Then, as the ball was nearly in front of him, he heard someone in the stands say loudly, "On that coward, he's supposed to jump."

John knew that if he leaped at that time, he would miss the pass, and it would bounce harmlessly off his fingertips.

Instead, John risked taking one more stride before leaping horizontally. He reached the ball just before it would have skidded off the ground. He fitted his hands underneath the ball and held onto it as his body skimmed across the grass, coming to a stop a few yards from where he had caught the ball.

John knew that the play was dead after he made the reception, because he lay on the ground, unlike professional football he did not have to be touched by a defender to be considered down.

The team came up and congratulated John on his great catch.

The quarterback then called a play in which John, lining up this time on the right side, would run the remaining 5 or 10 yards into the end zone, and catch the ball on a button-hook.

Instead, John jerked his body threateningly after the signals were called, and stood up directly. There was no defender within 7 yards of him. When he caught the ball that was thrown hard toward him, he had only to turn around and make the last few yards to the end zone to score a touchdown.

On another play, John ran downfield on the right side. He managed to deke his defender into thinking he would stop short for a pass reception. When the defender took the bait, John ran past him and headed toward the end zone.

John looked back over his shoulder and saw the pass releasing from the quarterback's hand, on a low enough trajectory that the eluded defender could still jump and knock it down.

John slowed down abruptly and moved backward toward the ball. He tried to look innocent as he began to stretch his hands toward the ball. The pass had not yet gone over the defender's head.

Just as the pass was going over the defender's head, the defender twisted around and broke his stride, trying to get a bead on the ball's location. The timing was just right for the ball to go past him as he was doing so.

Now the tough part was for John to catch it, since he was somewhat out of position to grab it, having gone backward and having cut his stride.

As the ball neared him, John jumped forward laterally, the ball reached his hands just as he was fully extended. John grabbed it.

Fearing that the impact with the ground would shake it loose, John spun in mid-air toward his right, landing on his back. It looked like a circus catch, but under the circumstances, it was the only way John could imagine making the reception.

On another play, with the same beginning, John did not have to worry about a defender knocking the ball down, because there was no defender in sight. The pass came in as he was nearing the goal line, but John did not extend his arms immediately in its direction.

Instead, John waited until the ball passed nearly completely before him, choosing only at the last moment to reach out for it, with his left hand on the top and the right hand below.

Someone in the stands had yelled, 'Catch it!' when the ball first neared him and when John turned his head from the left to look directly before him.

John felt that this was the safer approach to catching the ball, since a thrust of hands backward toward the ball would have put equal and opposite force against the in-coming ball, where snatching it as it went by him meant putting both hands and ball in the same direction for a smoother catch.

Chapter 17
Place-Kicking

John crossed over. He was in a pale room when he made out the figure of Jesus passing by. Jesus said, "He'll be with you in a few minutes," through a half-smile.

St. Peter next entered the room. He drew up a chair and directed some questions to John.

"You did most of the place kicking for your team, did you not?" He asked.

Not understanding the point of the question, John related to Peter some of his recollection from that day, starting with his lining up for the extra point after the catch where he landed face down in the end zone.

Unlike the other attempts he had made that day, John sensed that the opposition had a good angle on blocking his kick. He stood directly behind the holder, unlike the previous attempts, at which he had come from the holder's side soccer-style.

Just before the snap was made, the holder asked him quickly how to hold the ball. John remembered saying, "Same way."

The snap came back and the holder put it into the tee, tilting slightly back toward John, with the laces facing the scrimmage line. John had just enough time to put his foot into the ball, before the opposition broke through the line to come crashing toward him.

Another second later and the kick would have been blocked. Instead, it sailed true through the goal posts.

John had signaled that this extra point and the next were to be his last plays of the game.

Earlier in the game, on a kick-off, John had huddled momentarily with the players on the left side of the ball, as he approached placing it on the tee. John told them that, on the clap of his hands, they were to swing toward the right side of the ball. They inferred that he was going to attempt an on-side kick.

Confirming their assumptions, John placed the ball horizontally on the tee, rather than the standard semi-vertical rest in the tee. He then walked deliberately back to begin his kicking motion.

While he did so, the opposing team conferred among themselves as to how they would cover the expected on-side kick.

John clapped his hands and watched the players on the left file smoothly toward the right side. The players on the right side had no idea what was going on.

Finally, the last player on the left drew near the ball. John had been trudging as slowly as he could toward the ball, to allow the players on his left to get to the right, but this last player was taking too long.

John almost had to stop to let him get past but he knew that doing so would draw a 'delay-of game penalty'. His decision was to take two steps in exactly the same territory to let the slow player get by, without seeming to have stopped.

Finally, when his path to the ball was clear, John started his kicking motion. The opposing team saw no players on the kicking team's left side, so they all shifted to their left, to face them on the kicking team's right.

One defender stayed in the center to guard against any shenanigans from the wily kicker.

John moved his kicking foot straight toward the ball. He did not have to generate much momentum because by this time, it was evident to everyone that this was going to be a short kick.

John twisted his right foot slightly toward his right as it neared the ball. Without giving the center defender an opportunity to adjust his location, John sent the ball spinning upward and outward toward his left and down-field, in the area then completely vacated by players on both sides.

He knew that the rule on on-side kicks required the ball to travel 10 yards downfield before being touching by the kicking team. He ran to the location he judged to be where the ball would land, and waited patiently as the center defender came rushing in his direction.

John turned enough in his place to put his right leg between the ball and the on-coming defender, just as the ball landed about 10 yards downfield. He reached down and caught the ball, but moved it an extra 3 inches downfield before pinning it to the ground, just out of reach of the defender.

The whistle blew for a downed play and the defender broke his speed just enough to prevent breaking John's ankle when he fell into it. John had completed the on-side kick singlehandedly.

On a kick-off after an exciting touchdown in which one of his teammates had made a great play, John was late in getting an opportunity to congratulate the teammate.

All his teammates had crowded around the player to get a chance to tell him how great the play was, but after making the extra point, John had to take the tee and the ball downfield to do the kick-off.

John set the ball up in the tee and was just about to go back to begin his kicking motion when his emotions overcame his judgment, and he went to the right side where the exuberant teammate was setting up on the line to cover the kick downfield.

John rushed over, clasped the players hand in both of his hands, and told him, "Great play!" The ref threw the flag and penalized his team 5 yards for delay of game.

John again spoke to the left side of his downfield cover line. "Don't go, stay here," he said.

Then, after he placed the ball in the tee 5 yards back from where he had set it before, John said to his teammates on the right side, "Stay here, don't go!"

The teammates muttered to themselves, "Another on-side kick." The expectant opposing team readied themselves to rush toward the ball whichever direction it took. They were not going to be duped on a kick-off again.

Instead, John came running to the ball and jumped half-way up as he neared it. He heard his coach on the sideline say, "Now what's he doing?"

John reached his kicking leg down and started the motion before he had reached the apex of his jump. As he did so, he leaned forward somewhat, until his head was nearly over the ball.

Then, John swung his kicking leg hard into the ball. His follow-through nearly took him spinning in the reverse direction.

Rather than fall awkwardly on his rump, John deliberately drew his legs back to face the kickoff line—all before landing from his half-jump.

When he landed, John looked up. The ball was carrying far above and beyond the last line of the receiving team. It carried beyond the goal posts and the playing field.

It did not come to rest until it had reached the track surrounding the football field. John did not do the math on how far he had kicked the ball.

A teammate who did not appreciate John's antics passed him as they went to the sidelines to set up their defensive positions on the next series. Unlike his comment after John had been penalized for delaying the game (Great job—now we have to run an extra 5 yards!), the teammate said, "Great! Now they get the ball out on the 20-yard line."

John just rolled his eyes.

On what was to be his last significant play of the game, although his coach had told him to run to the side-line after kicking the ball off, John disobeyed the order and went down the middle to help to cover the kick.

John weaved in and out among the return team's blockers, and maintained a steady gait as he neared the return man. He saw that a teammate had already put an arm around the returner but was having trouble bringing him down.

John drew his helmet into the returner's helmet on his right side, and with his teammate on the returner's left, they were able to bring him down.

John thought that the signals he had given his coach, about having two last plays in him, had been seen by his teammates. After that kick-off, John expected to be taken out of the game, but instead his captain huddled the team quickly to call defensive signals.

John did not have time to get to the sideline. He stood in his position in the huddle, as the captain called the same defensive signals he had been calling all game long. Instead of taking his position on the field after the huddle however, John raised his left hand and whistled.

His coach knew what this meant. The substitute came in to replace him. John saw him coming and ran off, although he saw the offensive line approaching the line of scrimmage.

They would normally have been caught in the middle of a substitution with too many players on field, had it not been for the Paterson State quarterback. He waited before beginning to call signals, as a sign of respect for John, waiting for him to get off the field before starting the play.

Chapter 18
Quarterbacking

His assailants had forgotten to check John's pockets for a cell phone. Mary determined his location by the side of the road through a device on their cell phones keeping track of each other. She drove to the location where his body was slumped in the dark by the side of the road.

As fourth in the team's depth chart for quarterbacks, John had not expected to play there. When called upon, he knew that the defensive rush would be the biggest challenge to completing passes, and that going to the air would be the only way they could hope to catch up.

He used this to try to gain sympathy from St. Peter.

On one particular third down, as all his receivers had been sent to the left side, John knew that his right side would be open. Although, that was good as far as avoiding interceptions or pass deflections from defenders was concerned, that was not so good as far as having open receivers—or any receivers, for that matter—on that side.

Time was running out. The defender was rushing his way. John was unconvinced that he could elude him on one side or another. Just as the defender was reaching him, John lofted a pass upward and outward in the direction of an area about 5 yards diagonally upfield from where his right end had lined up.

The referee immediately threw a flag as there was no receiver in the area. The defender had seen his team flagged enough that day for roughing the kicker with late hits, so he let up and did not do anything more than brush John lightly when he arrived.

John braced himself and when he received little impact from the rusher, he ran around him. The defender tried to adjust his body to cut John's path off but he was already gone.

John ran downfield far enough to get past the slow-arriving ball. When it finally came down, John had to reach back to catch it about waist high. John pulled it in and covered it with both arms as he ran downfield far enough to make the first down.

Just as he had done so, two defenders came and took him down. John was light enough to be suspended long enough for them to strip the ball from him, but he took a knee to end the play before they could do so.

On another play, as the defenders were rushing in toward him in the middle, John had just enough time to release the ball in a high trajectory just over the center-line, as he had called for his receiver to look for the ball just about where the middle linebacker normally plays.

John was taken down by late-arriving defenders, but saw his receiver looking back as he had just reached the designated location for the pass reception. John signaled, "Up!" and called out the same thing, as he fell to the ground. The receiver gathered in the ball and was tackled shortly after making another first down.

On one play when they needed less than 5 yards for a first down, John saw that a defensive player had jumped offside but had not made contact with the offensive line. He tried to shorten the signals and call for an immediate hike. The defensive player did not retreat.

Then, John realized that the center was not going to hike the ball unless he called the signals in normal sequence. He shouted them out in a single breath, took the hike, and was awarded an offsides-penalty against the defender, giving his team a first down.

Once, John called a play in which his receiver was to run to the far upper corner of the end zone to draw his defender with him to the right side. John told the receiver to break sharply back in the same direction without touching the defender to avoid any type of pass interference call.

Then, John said to expect the ball to be thrown slowly just before the goal post, so that the receiver would have to jump to catch it.

The receiver followed directions completely. In the end zone, as he was breaking free from his defender, without touching him, the receiver began to gather speed, running back toward the goal post.

John lofted his laziest pass of the day toward the right side of the goal post, high enough that it took a strong leap from the receiver to catch the ball before landing in-bounds. The result was a touchdown.

After the defensive goal line stand, where he had run down a player who had run back one of his teammates' fumble recoveries the length of the field, John pulled his jersey part-way out of his pants to enable his next trick-play.

In the huddle, he told his end to take his time gaining separation from the scrimmage line, but to get sure he got behind the defensive secondary. The main call was for a fake run up the middle using his standard half-back on a fake hand-off.

When the snap was made, John turned away from the line of scrimmage and faked the handoff to the half-back. He pivoted around as if to watch how the runner was doing; as he did so, he used his left hand to tuck the ball inside his shirt.

John made an upward motion with both of his arms, as if following through after the hand-off. Only after the defensive cornerback had been lured far enough in toward the middle did his end break loose.

John led him nicely for a short pass that turned in to an 85-yard touchdown, then a school record for a play from scrimmage.

Chapter 19
Dirty Playing

John was trying to ingratiate himself with St. Peter by going on to tell him about his experiences as quarterback. He started with his thought process on that particular day.

Realizing that his experience as a quarterback had not impressed St. Peter, to emphasize his daring, John talked about the time the starting quarterback for Paterson State had been moving the ball at will. Seeing the quarterback look in the other direction for a receiver on that side to get open, John left his receiver and ran across the field. He deliberately timed his impact with the quarterback to occur just after the quarterback had released the ball.

John adjusted his motion to hit the quarterback in the shoulder joint of his throwing arm. He did not let up on his momentum, even though he knew it was too late to affect the pass, until the two hit the ground.

John effectively drove the shoulder on the quarterback's non-throwing arm into the ground as he drove the shoulder joint from the other side.

That put the quarterback out of the game.

This story did not impress St. Peter, even when he told him about a Paterson State player later trying to retaliate by kneeling over John as he hit the ground. No matter how he twisted or turned, the opposing player could counter his motion.

To gain St. Peter's sympathy, John said that he had feigned unconsciousness and let his arms fall limp by his sides. Breathing shallowly, John closed his eyes except for a narrow slit in one of them.

Just then, John saw the Paterson State player raise his fist high to deliver a blow to his face. John closed both eyes and waited a second or two.

When he thought he couldn't wait any longer, John shifted his head to the side and felt the opposing player throw all his weight into the punch.

Unluckily for the opponent, the fist missed John entirely and hit the dirt below where his head had been. The opponent shrieked in pain. Before he had a chance to remove the fist from the ground, John reached behind him and put his hands on the opponent's broken hand, pinning it to the ground.

In a flipping motion, John lifted the opponent over his body and threw it entirely on the ground above where his head had been.

John let go of the fallen player and rose to his feet. Another defender was rushing his way.

This time, John did not wait to act defensively. He rose a left fist to his shoulder, and when the opposing player neared him, he shot it in below the opponent's face mask, landing a strike on his mouth.

The impact dropped the player to the ground, enabling John to walk to the huddle for the next play.

Still later in the game, John was playing right cornerback when a power sweep was developing in his direction. He looked up to see the lead blocker attempting to conceal a hunting knife inside his left forearm. John pretended not to see it but sauntered brashly in the direction of the blockers.

He was seeing no help from his teammates at that time. He made a motion as if he were going to rush the blockers toward the back of the team leading the ball-carrier. When he saw the lead blocker adjust his direction to try to confront him, John stepped forward deliberately to kick him in the groin.

The crowd gasped as the blocker dropped the knife and fell to his knees in pain.

John reached down and picked up the knife—the same knife later to be found that the intruder had used to gain entry to his house that Christmas Eve.

John felt both sides of the knife to assure himself that it was not double-edged. Then he twisted the knife so that the sharp edge was inward and the dull edge was extending outward.

John drew the fallen blocker toward him by placing his free left hand on top of his helmet. He took the knife and slid the dull edge strongly against the neck of the fallen blocker. The blocker thought his throat had just been slit and he reached for his neck with both hands.

John held the knife high, and threateningly, as he walked toward the other blockers, who were then fanning out in fear of being cut. When they had opened enough space for him to run between them, John twisted his body backward and looked for help from the sideline.

His head coach walked up the sideline far enough to be within tossing range. John turned the knife backward and flipped it, handle-first, to the coach, who caught it cleanly.

John returned to the task of taking out the ballcarrier. The lead blocker was still on his knees on the ground. John latched onto the ball-carrier by the shoulder-pads and twisted him around so that the ball popped free.

By this time, they had gotten close enough to the goal line that John waited until he popped across the line before standing there to grasp the ball on the bounce.

John wanted credit for a touchdown, but did not think he could advance the ball after recovering it. Unfortunately, the ref had called the play dead when the runner's forward motion was stopped, midway through John twisting him backward.

On the sideline afterwards, John admired the curvature of the knife when given the opportunity by two of his teammates who were holding it after the coach had entrusted them with it.

After he had done so, instead of returning it politely to them, he threw it point-first into the ground about 7 feet from where they were standing. It was not there later in the game, when John, incensed by some of the misconduct on the field, returned to use it.

Sensing that St. Peter was not impressed by these acts of bravery and compassion, John elaborated on his errors in judgment to induce a sense of humility. From time to time, having been knocked down with an opponent, he had extended his hand in the opposing player's direction to help his opponent up.

St. Peter interrupted him to take the position that perhaps he wasn't entitled to heaven. He raised the occasion when John extended his hand to an opponent, the opponent responded by attempting to tug his arm downward, and John twisted his forearm away to free his arm.

Then John kicked his fallen foe in the groin before he got up. Realizing that the referee would call him for unsportsmanlike conduct unless he did something, John quickly jumped over the foe and landed on the other side.

John looked back as if innocently determining what was causing his opponent to shriek.

The ref looked away from the play on the other side of the field and looked toward John and the fallen opponent.

Since he saw nothing to suggest that John was the culprit, or indeed that there was any misdeed at all, the ref did not call a penalty.

Shortly afterward, he told John, between plays, that he did not know what John had done, but if he caught him doing it again, he would throw him out of the game.

St. Peter suggested that John had used the refs to his own advantage. Once on defense, he was struck across the left side of the helmet by a fist from the spread end on his side, just before the quarterback threw the ball in another direction.

After the next huddle, John told Johnson, doubling as a defensive back, to tell the ref that the end was hitting him when he came off the line. The ref watched as the end again brazenly struck John across the left side of the helmet before the ball was thrown. The ref immediately threw the flag, stopped the play, ejected the player, and penalized Paterson State 15 yards for a personal foul.

Chapter 20
Defensive Play

St. Peter told John that he would have to wait it out in Purgatory, where unexpectedly he was confronted by the Prince of Darkness himself. Meanwhile, Mary tried to revive John's lifeless body by the side of the road.

Satan told him that he could get him out sooner if John explained some things about his infamous day on the field.

In doing so, the Devil hoped to gain enough incriminating information from John to influence St. Peter to send him down to the Netherworld altogether.

One ambiguous play came when John wanted to delude the quarterback into believing that he had lost track of his receiver deep in the end zone. John took an extra step toward his left to give the quarterback an open lane for a pass to the receiver.

Then, as he saw the quarterback wind up for a throw, John reversed his direction by spinning to his left. He had just enough time to dive into the passing lane and tip the pass high over the receiver's head, out of bounds.

Satan asked him if John had expected one of the Paterson State players standing near-by to take a cheap shot at him after he had fully extended on the pass-deflection. A blow delivered with a shoulder or upper arm would have sent him sprawling awkwardly toward the ground at full speed.

John said he didn't remember but recalled that all the Paterson State players downfield had stepped aside and let him continue toward the goal post after tipping the ball.

John thought of his feelings as he looked up to see the goal posts coming his way. He had no chance to correct the angle he was taking, or to slow up the pace of its approach.

He thought of something an architecture-student friend had told him. The strongest figure in the world is that of an egg because its uniform curvature distributes shock and pressure evenly throughout its surface.

John arched his shoulders back as far as he could before making contact with the goal post. As he did, he let his back relax, so that the body rolled onto the stationary goal post by flopping with both ends toward its extremities.

Not wanting to force things too quickly, John grabbed the goal post, supporting his weight with his arms along, while he assessed his condition and whether he had snapped his spinal cord in the collision.

After taking a long breath, he realized that he was felt no pain and unwrapped his arms from the goal post.

The Devil wanted to take credit for that development, but John knew it was deceit.

"What's your point?" John asked him.

Beelzebub asked him about another play near the goal post. John made a last-second lunge, again going airborne— this time not in the direction of a post but more underneath it. He intercepted the pass, but again was at the mercy of the Paterson State players standing near-by.

Since John had not touched down yet, the play was not dead. One of the opposing players dealt him an upward blow.

John was vulnerable in this position, directly under the cross-bar of the goal post.

John came partly down when he was struck again in an upward blow. This time, his feet swung high enough for him to wrap them above the top of the cross-bar.

John swung himself once, twice, and then up into a sitting position on top of the cross-bar. He held the ball high in the air, defiantly proclaiming that he was alright.

The ref finally came over and told him to get down.

"Do you know who helped keep you from serious injury that time?" The Devil asked.

John remembered lifting his leg over the crossbar, shoving off, letting himself drop to the ground. He denied that the Devil deserved any credit for that result.

Chapter 21
The Abduction

The Devil continued his examination of John. "Isn't it true that he drew some criticism for showing off at various points in this game? Wasn't at least some of this criticism warranted?"

John defended by saying that Lucifer felt that he was gaining the type of record needed to have John sent to Hades instead of waiting his time out in Purgatory.

John came back to life just as the Devil realized that his case for Hades wasn't strong enough yet to assure that he would spend the rest of his eternity there.

Seeing that he was getting nowhere in his interrogation of John, the Devil asked him about the time that a student he had met while volunteering in the student newspaper's Business Department had introduced him to her roommate.

His friend had always been very upbeat. When she invited other volunteers to her apartment for drinks, they played Dr. John, the New Orleans jazz pianist and vocalist who was way ahead of his time in 1970.

Betty introduced John to her roommate, Bernadette, at a college mixer later in the year. She left the two alone to become acquainted. Betty was always playing matchmaker.

Bernadette and John haltingly attempted a conversation but the line of talk was too predictable for a college mixer. As the silence between subjects became too awkward, John asked Bernadette to dance. She declined.

John tried to establish rapport with her but Bernadette wasn't interested in small talk.

Bernadette wanted to go back to the dorm southeast direction of the dining center where the mixer was being held. John asked if she would like him to walk her back but Bernadette declined.

John responded to the Prince, telling him that as he recalled it, this is the way it developed.

John went back to his dorm and gathered up a few things to take with him to the newspaper office. Even at that late hour on a Friday night, there was still plenty of paperwork and accounting to do if he wanted to get a jump on the next week's activities.

This was a relatively safe college campus in Northeastern Washington, D.C. John had thought about insisting that he walk her to the dorm, but he had just met Bernadette and didn't want to seem pushy, in case he got a second chance some other time.

As John remembered it, he was counting on sleeping late the next Saturday morning. As he was passing from the pathway that led to the campus' main parking lot, a black sedan pulled up and the driver rolled down the window.

John did not recognize him.

The driver let John see the passenger in the middle of the front seat next to him. John could tell it was Bernadette.

As he was saying 'hi' to Bernadette, she said, "John, help me."

John asked, "What's the matter?"

Bernadette responded, "These guys grabbed me."

John asked the driver, "What's going on?"

The driver said, "We saw you talking to her in the mixer. We thought you might want to see her later."

John said, "What did you do, kidnap her?"

The driver said, "Well, I wouldn't exactly call it kidnapping."

John said, "Well, did she get in the car on her own?"

The driver said, "Well, I wouldn't exactly say that either."

John was becoming tense. He decided to try another tactic. He started walking away from the car as if he was ending the conversation and continuing on his way.

The driver offered an explanation. "We thought if you wanted to play with her, we could get her for you, and we would be asking a favor from you in return."

John asked, "Are you guys nuts? What are you talking about?"

The driver explained, "If you were to join our fraternity, we could let you have her, and everything would be fine."

By this time, John was able to get a better view of the fellow on the other side of Bernadette in the front seat. He was burly enough that John didn't think he could fight both of them without Bernadette in the middle getting hurt.

John tried another tactic. He thought he would use reverse psychology. He wanted to try to convince the guys that he was going to join their fraternity, talk them into releasing Bernadette, and he would definitely not be joining the frat.

He asked them, "What fraternity is that?"

The driver responded, "SBK."

John was struck by the irony. Of all the fraternities on campus, the one he had most been interested in joining was SBK—until this time. He was suddenly no longer interested in SBK at all.

He answered, "SBK? That's a pretty cool frat. I went to a mixer there. You guys have a pretty good house."

John could discern in the faint glow of the overhead parking lot light that the driver was skeptical. He thought that perhaps his sudden switch of interest might have been too soon, and too much.

John decided to focus on Bernadette. He said, "What are you going to do with her? You can't expect her to go with me now."

Bernadette found her voice again, and said, "You can count on that. You guys are all in trouble. You won't be getting out of this."

John, having only just met Bernadette about an hour earlier, was unconvinced that she wasn't part of the frat boys' attempt to convince him to join SBK.

John decided to continue his reverse psychology and act as if he was joining the boys' plan.

John said, "Yeah, I'll join your frat but you gotta let her go first."

The driver said, "You heard her. If we let her go, we're going to be in trouble."

John said, "Well, you can't exactly keep her. If you let her go now, you might be in less trouble than if you hold her longer."

The driver said, "We're not going to get into any trouble at all."

John tried to ignore the ominous implication of that statement. He acted as if he were hatching a plan to 'get them all out of this', although he had not agreed to do any harm to Bernadette and was trying to gain her release.

"I got it," John said. "We just all drive back to Zimmerman and when we get there, we let her out, and if she screams or something, or tries to 'rat us out', we'll just deny it. It'll be her word against ours."

The driver was even more skeptical now. He said, "What's to keep you from backing up her story, once we let her go and you're free?"

John said, "Well, I'm going to be free however you play it."

Bernadette again opened her mouth. "None of you guys are going to be free very long when I go to the cops."

John thought this was a perfect opportunity for him to finish the work on his reverse psychology. He said, "Wow, she's a mouthy one, isn't she?" The driver agreed with a nod of the head.

John was wishing someone else would be walking across the parking lot, so that he could enlist help in freeing Bernadette. When no one came by, he thought he might have to try to wrestle the keys to the car away from the driver by punching him in the face or by lunging into the car.

The driver seemed to read John's mind. As John inched closer to the car, the driver eased the car away from him, so that it always was over a yard away from John.

John decided that the tactic of trying to overwhelm the driver, even if he could get the element of surprise, would be too risky. He thought he better stay with the strategy of using reverse psychology.

If he could get the confidence of the guys in the car, he might be able to catch them off guard and gain an avenue of escape for Bernadette.

Yet John couldn't believe this was happening. He decided to gain the boys' confidence, if possible.

He said to the driver, "You guys ain't gonna rape her, are you?"

The driver gave a surprised expression. "No, that's not our style."

"Well, what are going to do with her?" John asked.

The driver said, "I don't know, we'll think of something."

John was getting desperate. He tried to gain the upper hand in the situation by stating, "Well, if you don't rape her, nobody's going to believe that you just grabbed her to try to convince me to join your fraternity."

Bernadette chimed in, "Nobody's going to rape me!"

John tried to even out the tension. "Bernadette, just be quiet. Let me try to set this straight."

Then, after some more thought, John suggested, "Why don't you just let them rape you? It would be better than getting killed."

At that point, the rider on the other side of Bernadette raised his hand to show that he was holding a gun.

John saw it for the first time.

The lad gave a wicked snicker and said something nearly inaudible, but sounding like, "Yeah, we might kill her anyway."

At that, John decided to drop the psychology. He said, "You guys gotta let her go. Whatever she accuses you of, I'll back your story. Just don't hurt her."

"No," the driver said. "We don't trust you."

John retorted, "Hey, just a minute ago you were offering her to me to get me to join your fraternity. What happened?"

The driver said, "Well, I'm thinking that wasn't such a good idea."

"You guys been drinking?" John asked.

The passenger on the other side of Bernadette said, "Yeah, let's just go."

John couldn't believe that no one, including a security officer, had come by in all this time. As the car eased away from him, John realized that he needed to do something fast.

As the car got closer to the parking lot light in the center of the lot, John could see Bernadette start to struggle with the guys. Her arms rose and she was trying to hit someone.

The passenger on her right raised his hand and took it down in the direction of her head. John then knew this was a real abduction.

The girl was not just playing along in order to assist them in getting him to join their fraternity.

John put on a burst of speed to get near the car as it was passing under the light. In the distance of about 20 feet by this time, he could make out the license plate number on the car—24XFZU15.

He knew he had to call the police as the car sped off through the parking lot and took the one exit available, left toward Michigan Avenue.

John wanted to know what this had to do with his fate after passing. Satan said that he had a different version. If his version is worse than John's, maybe John didn't deserve to be in Purgatory after all. Maybe he deserved to be in Hell.

Pars Siete

Chapter 22
Escape

Satan told John that he would agree to an early release from Purgatory if John went back and cleared up the account of what happened that night when Bernadette was killed. He accused John of having selective memory.

Mary was getting nowhere with reviving John. She dialed 911.

John realized that what he had experienced had not been a dream. He had already tried once before to tell everyone exactly what had happened, but no one had believed him.

John had gone to the Tower office and had locked the door to the business office behind him. When he heard someone open the exterior door next to his office door, he turned off the lights and sat in the dark, waiting.

One voice said to another, "Nobody in here. The call came from the Tower office. Let's try the News office down the hall."

At that moment, John realized that those entering the Albert Hall at that late hour weren't the ones who had kidnapped Bernadette. Still, he sat in darkness at his desk, not wanting to get involved.

After the stillness lasted for about ten minutes, John thought it safe enough to turn the lights back on. He finished his work and went to his dorm room.

On the way, he relived the experience from the time the car had left the McMahon parking lot. Repeating the license plate number to himself as he hustled down the walk toward Albert Hall, he passed a fellow student with his date, but by then, it was too late to solicit help in stopping or even delaying the abduction.

Reaching the Tower office, he picked up the phone to the campus operator and blurted, "24XFZU15. Write that down." When the operator said he didn't know what John was talking about, John said, "Connect me to the campus security." The operator was still confused and rejected the request.

Finally, in frustration, John asked the operator to connect him with the D.C. police. He said it insistently, and within moments the dial tone was answered by a dispatcher.

Again, John said, "24XFZU15. Please write that down."

The dispatcher asked, "What's this all about?"

John said he would tell her as soon as she wrote the number down.

The dispatcher said, "I got it. 24XFZU15. Now tell me what happened."

John related the entire story and when he was finished, the dispatcher asked his name. Suddenly, overtaken by fear, John had hung up the phone.

John went about clearing up his duties at the Tower Business office and at his schoolwork. Shortly before the campus went on to December Holiday Break, the word came out. Bernadette had been found dead.

John went back to his dormitory shortly afterward, not knowing the rest of the story. In confusion, he did not come forward with his part of the events. He justified it by thinking that nothing he could say or do would bring Bernadette back.

A few weeks in the spring semester, one of the writers said that she had heard that a certain Phillip, who had been arrested for murdering Bernadette, had 'escaped from St. Elizabeth's'. St. Elizabeth's was the mental institution in the northwest District of Columbia, south Maryland area.

John took solace in knowing that someone had been taken into custody for this wrong. It made sense to him that the perpetrator would have been assigned promptly to a mental institution.

John did not hear anything more about the events, except for attending a campus memorial for the deceased student, until the spring, when there was a meeting of students with administrators to quell some unrest on a number of topics.

The issue of the lack of campus security and the unease regarding the resolution of the investigation into Bernadette's murder arose. The students expressed understandable frustration, until John became increasingly uncomfortable, as Betty, the friend who had introduced him to Bernadette, complained that the investigators had not yet even found out who had placed the call to the police.

Instinctively, John said, "What difference does that make? It won't bring Bernadette back." Some of the students nodded in agreement but Betty and some others were astonished.

"Of course, it makes a difference. It makes a difference to her family and to those of us who loved her."

Again, John made a statement he regretted almost as soon as it had been made. "Why don't you leave the guy alone? He obviously doesn't want to get involved and you should respect that he called it in. I think you should leave him alone."

Then as everyone looked suspiciously at John and a pause became unbearable, John rose and went forward to the front of the meeting, took up the microphone, and said, "Well, I might as well admit it. I was the one who called the police that night."

A gasp went up from the crowd, and Betty, sitting nearby, said, "You killed her! I mean you were part of the group that killed Bernadette."

John looked directly into Betty's eyes and said, "No, I didn't kill her and I had nothing to do with her death." Then he went on to tell the story of the McMahon Hall parking lot encounter that followed his conversation with Bernadette after Betty had introduced them.

People looked at him in astonishment and nothing further was said, other than Betty's question, "What fraternity?"

John answered, "SBK."

Betty had said, "That fits. That guy who was arrested was a member of SBK fraternity."

Hoping to ease some of the tension in the room, John said in a conciliatory tone, "I remember thinking that was ironic. If there was any fraternity I had thought about joining, it would have been SBK."

Then Betty again accused him, "You were in on it. It was part of a frat prank."

"No," John assured her and the audience. In his story, he left out the same accusation that had been made by Bernadette (and his denial) that fateful night.

Finally, John got to his feet and began to leave the room. As he reached the door, one of the college administrators said, "Well, I never thought I would see this day. A student at CUA making up a story to cast blame on one of our fine fraternities in order to throw dirt on an innocent institution."

John responded, "That's exactly why I didn't come forward earlier. Nobody would believe it." Then he put his hand on the bar to open the exit door and left without anything else being said.

Chapter 23
More Escapes

"Oh, so what?" John asked. "I have told all of this to the school administration and my classmates before, and nothing ever came of it," he said. "The police never even interviewed me."

Lucifer said, "You weren't such a hero then, and you aren't one anymore."

Mary explained to the paramedics what happened. They contacted the police to see what could be done to track the assailants.

As an adverse character reference, the Devil reminded John of the time he was on Thanksgiving vacation in his junior year of college when Marvin asked him to stay with him at his home in Newark.

The day after the holiday, Marvin announced that he was going to see a mutual friend of theirs, Chelsea, who had transferred from their college to Jackson State campus of Tufts University.

John didn't know how familiar Marvin was with her, but he knew that he had gotten close to becoming intimate with her before she traded schools.

Interpreting Marvin's announcement as an invitation to come along, John asked to be included. He was partially playing along with Marvin's emotions, knowing that there would be nothing for him to do at Marvin's house while he was gone, unless he wanted to continue catching up with his schoolwork—a never-ending chore.

Marvin allowed it and the two went to visit Chelsea who was home from school at her parents' house in New Jersey.

Midway through their conversation, Chelsea suggested that they 'visit her at her dorm at Jackson State'.

John took that as a genuine offer to spend time with him if he came up to Boston for a visit, and made a secret pledge to himself to do so when the opportunity arose.

During the ensuing Christmas holiday break, without having announced his intention to anyone, John took the train up to Boston and used the MTA map to find his way to the Jackson State campus.

When he reached Chelsea's room, he was somewhat surprised that she wasn't there. She had always been something of a bookworm and he expected to see her up to her ears in cramming for semester exams.

John waited around in the hallway outside Chelsea's room, when the lady in the room next door opened her door and asked what he was waiting for.

John explained and they fell into a long chat, while he sat on his suitcase. She made an odd comment about ¾ of the way through, that she was surprised that 'Chelsea had a guy like you interested in her'.

John did not ask for further explanation.

Chelsea did arrive later that afternoon and was surprised that John had come to visit her. She let him in to her room and complained that, had she known he was coming up, she would have arranged for him to stay with George, a friend of hers.

They would have made plans to go to the museums and other things.

As it was, Chelsea had been intending to go home that very evening for a weekend. She was willing to cancel that plan but she needed to work out some of the alternative details to do so.

Suspecting that part of John's plan had been to stay with her, not with some friend of hers, Chelsea began to fret and try to decide what to do.

John decided to show some of his cards, beginning with a bottle of scotch that he had gotten from a liquor store in his neighborhood, although he was underage. John carried a false ID.

Rather than setting Chelsea at ease, this disclosure made her more nervous. She asked John, "Was that your plan? To get me drunk and then have your way with me?"

John didn't think it wise to concede that this had indeed been part of his plan. He had been fond of Chelsea since they first met in the freshman year. He blamed himself for letting her go when she said that she was thinking of transferring from his college.

In fact, he actually challenged her to go, saying that he didn't think she had the nerve to transfer.

John wanted to make sure that she had no regrets about anything, so he challenged her to make the transfer, saying that he didn't think she 'had to guts to do it'.

Had she failed to go through with the transfer, John thought that he would have her in his emotional control. She would have implied that she indeed did not have the courage to make a change in her life, but would be passive in pursuing a career.

John had been surprised that she did transfer.

As if the failure to deny the liquor part of his plan had not been enough, John then went off on asking Chelsea to look into the mirror and tell him what she saw. She just said, "A girl with a future."

John told her to continue looking at the mirror and he had a surprise for her. While she complained about the awkward treatment, he took off his clothes and piled into her bed. Then he told her she could look his way.

Chelsea acted somewhat surprised but continued the conversation. "What did you think you would find when you came up to visit me, a bunch of college students fornicating in the hallway?"

John admitted that he didn't have any expectations about anyone other than her when he departed on his visit to her campus. After a few flustered exchanges, John noticed that Chelsea, who had been sitting on the edge of the bed, was looking at his bare chest.

Wanting not to appear too forward, he took the sheet and pressed it against his chest, covering it.

Chelsea made her move. She told him to wait there, 'not to go anywhere', and she would be back after she made some contacts to decide what to do that weekend.

Suspecting a trap, John arose, dressed quickly, left her a note, and left via the stairway rather than the elevator.

Just as he was reaching the ground floor, he saw Chelsea leading a security guard, and saying, "Up this way." He had just enough time to step into a side hospitality-room as they swept past him and made their way up the elevator.

John realized that he had to get off the campus quickly.

John went to a coffee shop that was open late at night and ordered some doughnuts and coffee. He had made note of the time the train would be departing Boston that evening for the city where he was studying.

John knew that he had a few hours before he had to make his way to the train station.

John read from the book he had taken with him for the journey and wished he hadn't left the bottle of scotch in Chelsea's room with a note, 'Before studying international relations, you should learn something about personal relations first.'

John got into an extended conversation with a student at the coffee counter. As they were getting into a debate on the relative strengths of the professional and college football teams, a police officer entered and looked around.

John had changed jackets. What's more, he did not fit the description of the guy who had been in Chelsea's room. The police were looking for someone on the move, not seated at the counter of a doughnut shop.

The officer left to search elsewhere.

John decided that it was too risky to leave at that time for the train station. The police would be looking for him, on Chelsea's complaint to be headed toward the station.

When the time finally came, John got off the MTA red-line at the station before the train station and walked toward the train station, thinking that the police would be looking for him at the station closest to the Amtrak station.

His suspicions were confirmed as he approached the station, suitcase in hand. He saw an unusual amount of police activity around the station.

John decided against going into the waiting room and stood near a pillar outside. He heard an officer say to the conductor, "If you see anybody matching that description, let us know."

Thinking that this was too odd to be a coincidence, John waited until the train was just about to leave the station. Then he boarded the last car to become the only passenger on that car.

Still uncomfortable with being out in the open until the train had left the station, and not willing to explain his awkward attempt at seducing Chelsea to a stern Boston judge, he took his suitcase and crowded into the restroom at the back of the railroad car.

John turned the lock and held his breath. Not long thereafter, the conductor came by and tested the door on the restroom. Finding it locked, he asked, "Is there anyone in there?"

John gave no answer. The conductor looked through the keys on his keychain, and realized that he did not have one to open the restroom door. He tried a few keys to no success.

Meanwhile, John sat in complete silence, hoping that the train would start moving.

The conductor cursed under his breath and went out of the train car to the next car up. As the train left the station, John continued to hold his breath.

Finally, when it was underway and John estimated it had left Boston, he ventured out of the restroom and took a seat in the otherwise vacated car.

John was delighted to see a sign indicating that they were no longer in Massachusetts. Just then, the conductor returned to the car. He looked surprised to see John, who had placed his ticket for Washington, D.C. on the back of his seat.

The conductor clipped the ticket, asking him how long he had been there. He checked the restroom. Realizing it was too late to alert the police, the conductor grumbled to himself and went back up the train with a disappointed air.

John disembarked at the Washington station and went on his way. When he reached his apartment, he found his roommates smoking some pot.

John joined in. Vlad suggested that they drop some acid. Exhausted from his trip, John talked them down from a half-tab to a quarter-tab. He was just feeling the effects when they entered a movie theater.

John found himself seated with his friends in the eighth row of the theater when the movie began.

He had already seen *Apocalypse Now* before but he wasn't going anywhere.

John kept telling himself, "It's just a movie."

The effects of the hallucinogenic made it sure that he was in the jungle as the movie unfolded.

Vlad suggested afterwards that John should drive. John found the car key in his hand. His hand was too jittery to put the key into the slot to open the door.

When Vlad saw his difficulty, he suggested that Pete do the driving. Pete took the key. They made it home safely. John slept it off.

Chapter 24
Still More Escapes

The paramedics called for the medical examiner to meet them at the county hospital. On arrival, the examiner pronounced John dead from blunt force trauma.

"Okay," John said to Lucifer. "But I should get some credit for this one."

When John was a freshman, he was invited to go along with the seminarians from his home Catholic district (diocese) to a dinner sponsored by his home bishop, while he was in town for a national conference of bishops. Afterwards, he heard some of the upperclassmen discussing who was going to entertain the bishop privately later that night.

When someone suggested John, the common notion was that John was too young and uninitiated to be given that assignment.

The next morning, John was prevailed upon to join the same group for brunch. While they sat in the car waiting for the bishop and his assistant, the two seminarians who had discussed the bishop's playmate the night before, got into a discussion regarding what had happened after the dinner.

"Well, how did it go?" One seminarian asked.

The other responded, "It was terrible." Then after a long pause, the second added, "He better approve my request for a car after all that."

John fell out of contact with the seminarians after that, except that they crowded into a Volkswagen bug to go home for Christmas break a few months later. No further discussion of the bishop's proclivities was held, at least on that trip.

The next year, when the bishop was in town for the annual conference, John was too busy with student politics that even his parents were having trouble getting into touch with him. The following year, John was a walk-on on the school's club football team, and was either on the field, in the classroom, or sound asleep if the bishop's administrator had tried to reach him.

Finally, in the senior year, when the call came, John was doing nothing but studying and attending classes. He fielded the call.

A seminarian said, "John, we want you to attend the dinner when the bishop is in town."

John replied, "I can't really make it. I have to focus on my schoolwork. I need to get my grades up if I want to go to graduate school or law school."

"Law school? I didn't know you were thinking about law school," said the seminarian. "Wouldn't that be inconsistent with your pledge?"

John said, "I don't know what pledge you are talking about."

The seminarian said, "You know, the pledge to enter into the priesthood."

John replied, "I don't know that I pledged to go into the priesthood. I agreed to look over the various orders that are available for that type of vocation while I was here, but I didn't say definitively that I would enter any one if none of them appealed to me."

The seminarian said, "Well, the bishop and you can talk about that when you get together at the dinner."

John said, "I can't go to a dinner."

The seminarian said, "Well, it's your turn."

John responded, "My turn for what exactly?"

The seminarian was noncommittal, and the subject and telephone call was dropped.

Two months later, when he was once again back home for Christmas vacation, he got together with his high school mentor who had helped him select his classes for the first year of college, Fr. Xavier.

They made plans to go to the small parish outside town to which the priest was assigned, and celebrate New Year's Eve before the New Year's Mass expected the day after. Just to be on the safe side, John had invited his high school friend, Jose, to come with him.

When Fr. Xavier greeted them, he was surprised, but he agreed to take both John and Jose with him to the parish.

Once in the parish community center, John amused himself trying to play what few bars of the song, *By the Time I Get to Phoenix,* on the center's piano. The priest and Jose were taken up with preparing some artwork for the bishop's birthday, which was to be celebrated a few days later.

When John tried to join in the art-work, Fr. Xavier rejected whatever ideas or models he prepared. John turned to drinking some of the scotch that the priest had purchased on the way.

Finally, Jose and Fr. Xavier were satisfied with their product and the priest announced that it was time for bed. John took up a place on the blanket spread on the floor by the priest's bed and Jose lay next to him.

Before he had fallen asleep, he heard Fr. Xavier ask, "Which one of you boys is going to join me?"

After a slight pause, Jose replied, "I will," and he climbed into bed with the priest. John kept his eyes closed and tried to shut out the sound of two men making love in the bed a few feet away from him.

Nevertheless, John distinctly heard the groans and grunts of Jose as Fr. Xavier entered him with some pain. When it was finally over, John fell asleep, and no further word was said about it.

The next morning, John heard Fr. Xavier getting up and preparing to go into the chapel to say Mass on New Year's Day. At that time, New Year's Day was a holyday of obligation, as it happened to be the feast of the choosing of the infant Christ's name or His presentation to the synagogue in the area where he was being raised.

One of the parishioners raised the issue of his somehow having known or suspected that Fr. Xavier had entertained young men in his residence the night before the Mass.

Fr. Xavier was flustered and seemed at a loss for words to say. John spoke up, from his position in the last pew of the church.

"This is the House of God. Take your recriminations elsewhere."

The parishioner said, "That's one of them, who is he to attend this Mass, and who are you, Fr. Xavier, to celebrate it for us?"

By this time, Fr. Xavier had regained his composure. "Yes, I'm afraid he's right. If you have a problem with me, you should take it up with the bishop."

Fr. Xavier went on with the Mass, and when it was over, he and the boys returned to their home town by car. The conversation was awkward, but the priest said at one point, "Thank you for bailing me out in there. I wish I had thought of that, what you said."

John acknowledged the thanks and never again thought about becoming a priest after that.

Pars Ocho

Chapter 25
Wine Wasted

In rebuttal to the Devil, John brought up one of his finer moments as recompense.

As John grew up in the Midwest, wine in the 1960s meant little more than Maneschewitz on Thanksgiving morning (poured by an eager but otherwise loyal Falstaff beer drinker) or, later, in the 1970s Paul Masson pinot noir on special occasions like his older brother's return from law school. He taught his little brother to say 'pee no more', without the 'm'.

But as John attended San Francisco State University in fall 1974, he was nearing the end of the semester with an '0-fer' in dates.

John took a risk and bought two tickers to a George Harrison-Billy Preston-Ravi Shankar concert and asked his first choice, who was 'otherwise occupied'.

As he sat dejectedly at the table in the dining hall, wondering how to remedy this situation, a sprightly, athletic brunette sat down at the far end of the table. John opened with, "Are you from San Francisco?"

It wasn't much later that she was picking him up for the concert at the Cow Palace.

John had splurged on a nice corkscrew and bought his old, reliable Paul Masson pinot noir, when seeing the security at the gate, he pushed the bottle into the back of his pants, secured by his belt, upside-down to match the cleft and hidden by the shirt, sweater-vest and jacket he wore.

As they neared the gate, Susan went before him, and John watched the guard pat her down for contraband, on all the locations that he hoped to frequent in their later acquaintance. He shouted, "She doesn't have it, I do!"

He twisted halfway around and lifted his shirt to show the guard where the wine was. The guard let Susan go and took the bottle from John. Then he unceremoniously tossed it into a dumpster nearby.

As he turned his attention to the next in line, John looked longingly over the edge of the dumpster, but realized that the bottle was too far down for him to reach. Then the guard caught sight of him and shushed him off.

Susan and John had a good chuckle but his evening was nearly spoiled. He kept hearing the clank from the bottle landing in the dumpster, even as George sang, *My Sweet Lord.* He perked up as Harrison and Ravi Shankar did a duet of *While My Guitar Gently Weeps*, but afterwards, when he realized that he had nothing to continue the socializing, he was despondent.

Susan chivalrously stopped at a liquor store and purchased a bottle of brandy to them to enjoy later.

Months later, back in South Dakota, John eagerly opened a letter from her, answering his porous out-flowing of affection since that evening. It was a 'Dear John', and John was devastated. Somehow though, she worked into the closing a remark, "Watch out for the 1973 Charles Krug claret. Buy it whenever you can."

Years later, John was stocking up for a party to celebrate his 'First Annual *John Got Into Law School* occasion'. He went to the neighborhood distributor on Ocean Ave. near Phelan.

There was the 1973 Charles Krug claret. He bought a case of it and they made a serious dent in the case at the party.

Across the room, seated politely with her friend from City College, was the cheerful woman with the light flip wave on her bangs, who rented a room on the top floor of the house where John was renting a room on the ground level.

Years later, she was to become John's wife, constant companion, soul-and-inspiration, and mother of their two kids—who now prefers Zinfandel and Pinot Noir to claret.

Chapter 26
Flashbacks

Still seeking to make a case for mitigation of his sins, John tried to bring up other matters.

John was repeatedly bothered by flashbacks to his 1971 Football Club, even as he was studying in graduate school and canvassing for political organizations door-to-door years later. That club was best known for its aborted season, canceled after going 0–3 against St. Francis (NY), Georgetown, and Paterson State (NJ).

That doesn't even include the two preseason slaughter they suffered against the plebes at the Naval Academy and against a local high school team. But for John, the key memories that kept coming back to him decades later were these:

After chasing down a defensive lineman who had stripped the club's running back of the ball at the offensive goal line, John motioned to a teammate to carry over his helmet, which had flown off as he began his pursuit from the opposite sideline;

After a few tackles for losses, John motioned to the opposition's sideline, drawing his finger across his shoe tops, and flexed his hand in a 'Come on and try' movement.

After getting fouled on a completed drop kick for a 20-yard field goal, John stepped aside and clasped his hands above his head in a waterskiing signal that, "I'm OK."

After the crowd rose up to cheer when they made one of their rare touchdowns, John held his fist chest-level with thumb extended laterally, and made the motion one would use to carve a cut across wood or linoleum.

Then he opened his hand and imitated a sweeping motion toward the crowd, all as if to say, "Where were you earlier, when we were getting beaten pretty badly?"

After another touchdown, John raised his arms in typical jubilation, only to have the defensive end on that side knock him down with a slug to the face; John rose and quickly made the same gesture only to see this guy wind up for a second blow. This time, John was ready for it.

He ducked, stepped in, planted his fist dead-center in the guy's chest, saw him drop to his knees, gasping for breath with a suddenly pale complexion.

When Paterson State put its sub-third string quarterback in because of its long lead, John noticed his nervousness and got their coach's attention. He yelled, "Your QB!" He held out his hand, shaking. He yelled, "He's scared. Take him out on next play…" and he put his two fists together chest high, thumbs extended toward one another, and then bent the fists away from each other, as if breaking a stick. The coach replaced the quarterback on the next play.

John had been taught that if signaling for a fair catch, he had to extend his arm and move it forward and back. To catch the opposition off guard, he put his arm up but did not move it forward and back. This allowed him to advance the ball with a nice return while the defense watched.

Then on the next punt return, to draw a penalty from the punt coverage team, he signaled for a fair catch properly, but the coverage team apparently thought that, because he had been allowed to run after putting his arm in the air before, there must have been no fair catches allowed in that game. The lead cover man smothered him on his catch, but drew a penalty.

Once when the crowd showed its appreciation for some decent play despite being far behind on the scoreboard, John raised his arm and circled it around backward in a sardonic salute.

When John filled in at quarterback, his receivers and he had a code for 'going long' and another for 'breaking across the middle'. The former was for John to cut his finger across sideways, and the latter was to cast his arm in the forward direction—both the exact opposite of what the defenders would have thought.

The pass defending secondary never caught on to this, allowing the club to catch up on the scoreboard.

Chapter 27
Getting the Foot in the Door

Beelzebub in rebuttal brought up this episode for which John had never sought forgiveness.

Several years later, when John was in therapy, he was taken back to events he had suppressed in his consciousness. The first of these began with a telephone ring.

Bbbrring.

The phone rang just as he had finished supper. Staring blankly at the evening news, John knew what the phone call was. He had been dreading it all summer.

"John," his brother, Jed, said. "It's for you."

Gathering all his courage, John took the phone. "Guess who this is," the feminine voice on the line asked.

"Carol?" He asked playfully. She knew that John knew who it was.

Hearing the negative, John tried again, "Joyce?"

"Yeah," she said.

It had been a year since John had last talked with her. She had said she was an introvert and could not get along with an extrovert.

Considering that a compliment, John took off in his father's car, only to start crying on the way home. The rain was splattering on the windshield and the radio played *Abraham, Martin and John.*

Joyce called to congratulate John on his scholarship to college. John started to say "It was nothing," but he knew that it was more than that. He stood on the doorstep of a new chapter to his life, even as his classmates were being drafted to the Vietnam War.

John would see her twice more in the coming months— once at Christmas and then two summers later, when they buried her brother-in-law who had been killed in a car accident. "It was finished," she had said.

The next day, Joyce left for a local college, and John flew 1400 miles to a Washington, D.C. college. From the first day of school to the last, he would think of her daily.

Arriving at Dulles airport, John turned quickly to schooling. There was a young lady in the terminal that John knew from the local press; she was to be one of his classmates in college. John's only concern then was whether he would exceed the community's expectations for her.

His classmate, Mary Pat, entered speech and drama; John took philosophy as a major. He hoped to score at least one class with her.

When they finally found themselves in an English class together in their junior year, he realized how bright she was, how stupid he had been to be competitive with her, and how much he wanted to stay in philosophy. One of John's first male acquaintances in college was Gary Smith. He helped John out when times were rough psychologically.

John tried to keep up with him; both tried to keep each other from becoming too depressed.

Gary was from Southeast Washington, D.C.

John had heard this was a tough part of town.

Gary said that it wasn't too hard, if you grew up there.

Later on, Gary was instrumental in introducing John to Colonel Rafiq of the Blackman's Liberation Army (BLA). This was to become one of John's most memorable experiences.

BLA was composed of former drug addicts and pushers who were now in the process of cleaning themselves up. Some of them were just concentrating on kicking the habit, others were keen on pursuing the death of drug trade.

All were fully committed to ending the drug trade in Washington, D.C. They were not naïve. They carried pistols and kept bodyguards for protection.

The BLA was gaining ground. They had cut into the drug traffic to such an extent that the dealers had contracts out for the killing of its two top men, Col. Rafiq and Col. Hassan, who had taken up Islam in realization that much of the injuries suffered in the past had been the result of Western capitalism and culture.

The first near-hit took place at the BLA headquarters, with Col. Hassan as the target. John ditched the BLA that day. He had enough demons of his own to put up with.

The freshman year went smoothly, until a woman who worked with John at the college newspaper introduced him to one of her roommates, Bernadette. Bernadette was murdered that same evening.

The whole campus went into a security uproar. Fences were erected to halt the speedy flight of law-breakers. The security police were armed with guns and patrolled with Doberman pinschers. Meetings for student in-put on the situation were held across the campus.

Nevertheless, when a student mass was held to pray for Bernadette's soul, few people attended.

John's first reaction had been to analyze the dynamics of group involvement. He later reflected on it when reading Hobbes's political philosophy. All things take place in self-interest.

John remembered his first days of student organizing before college. Speaking in Dell Rapids, John had gathered the greatest response by contradicting Stokely Carmichael's invocation, 'Burn, baby, burn'.

Peace and justice could be achieved non-violently.

Later, when speaking at Washington High School, the only way he received any response was to bring up the Chinese curse, "May he live in interesting times."

The security concerns at his college eventually dissipated. John wrote in his college newspaper that this was not the time to go back on commitments to the neighboring community.

Eventually, it was learned that the primary suspect in Bernadette's killing was a mentally disturbed student at the college, not a resident of the neighborhood. The campus came short of embarrassment at their assumption that it hadn't been one of them.

Chapter 28
Fear and Loathing in the Nation's Safest Large City—A Liberal in the Police Academy

John's body was on the way to the undertaker while his spirit kept up the negotiations with Lucifer.

In rebuttal, the Prince of Darkness reminded John of the incident where he had misgivings about volunteering to go to the police academy with other Human Rights Commissioners. He had been on ride-alongs with two very decent police lieutenants over the past eighteen months. He expected the experience at the police academy to be equally dull.

John had been a liberal since the '60s. He was a high school senior when he read Jessica Mitford's essay on 'Why Liberals Hate Cops (and Vice-Versa)' in the *Atlantic Monthly* back in South Dakota, that hot bed of free-thinking.

On the other hand, his association with minorities at that time had been playing opposite some black youth in a basketball game on the junior varsity and watching the varsity play a team from one of the Indian reservations. So, he could be excused for 'not getting it'.

Then, in college in Washington, D.C., John saw some police tactics in controlling anti-war demonstrations that were less than tidy. He thought he had lived up to my reputation as being left-of-center by catching some tear gas at one of them.

So, as a Human Rights Commissioner, John was trying to get back into touch with his roots when community forums on the taser and other police practices made him realize that it was more than an academic exercise.

When elected chair of the HRC, he encountered resistance from the city manager's office, when trying to establish an agenda that wasn't restricted to promoting the law enforcement's viewpoint.

John also found that, were it not for the Santa Clara County Civil Grand Jury's findings on two occasions during his term as commissioner, there would not have been much attention given to anything the HRC had to say on the subject.

But there, John was before the City Council in June 2007, trying to spout off on what he had read in the Independent Police Auditor's 2006 year-end report and what IPA and HRC had written as their reports on the community forums.

His dry presentation included a criticism of the SJPD definition of 'racial profiling', that depends upon the contact, investigation, or other detention being based 'solely' on a suspicion aroused by the subject's race or ethnicity.

It would be an unimaginative officer who couldn't come up with some explanation that didn't at least branch off into another area of legitimate concern, although the initial contact might have been prompted by a report like, 'He was a black person on the street in Almaden Valley'.

So, when asked by Lt. Konn, the training officer in charge of the police academy, to put into words the questions that he had in the forefront of his mind when starting the experience, John thought of two:

"When a suspect is described in terms that include his or her race, how does the officer avoid just singling out that racial group when looking for someone like that?" And, "When an officer goes through a mall or some similar large public gathering place, does he or she think about the description of the suspects that are reported on the loose at that time, does he or she look for people considered likely to have been involved in types of criminal activity, or does he or she simply observe the people and their activity, and respond to the observations?"

A. Day One

John took out his camera-phone when Chief Davis made the rounds of those attending the academy, and snapped his picture just as he was approaching with hand out-stretched. It was as much to prove to himself that this was really happening, as it was to show Mary the latest trophy from his hunts.

Davis then introduced his four deputy chiefs, one of whom was covering a conference in Chicago for him 'so that he could be with us here tonight'.

The question came to mind immediately: "Do the chief and the deputy chiefs have marksmanship competitions?" Followed quickly by, "How recently have they fired their weapons?" and "Who was the best shot among them?"

John never got an answer to these questions.

The HRC commissioners were given releases to sign, and the vague explanation that they would be involved in a 'hands-on learning experience'. John's experience since kindergarten, preparing himself for physical contact with others in a group, kicked in.

He scanned his fellow academy attendees to rank them from least favorable contacts to least offensive contacts. He had the notion that some of them were doing the same thing.

John lined out the part of the release that said that it would be okay to make him the object of a taser demonstration. He had enough violence in his lifetime, growing up in a Norwegian Protestant ethic, heavy-handed enforcement environment. Escalating the discipline at his advanced age now seemed counterproductive.

At least, one of his fellow HRC commissioners had bragged that he had 'been tased' before. John left it up to him to re-volunteer.

After hearing some warm-up stories from officers lower in rank than the top brass, the commissioners were shuttled off to get ID badges, tour the facility, see the firing range and view a photo of an officer's injured hand. That accident had happened when he had forgotten to unload his weapon when cleaning it.

John and the HRC commissioners sat in on the midnight briefing that was given to the night shift before they went out in their patrol cars. Like them, he examined the skyline from the roof of the building. He was never able to ask questions like, 'Since when is that illegal'? and 'When was the last time a patrol car was stolen'?

John thought of the Neighborhood Watch meetings he had attended and the concerns about household break-ins. He asked one of the officers questions about gun registration. Does it have to be done at the police station? What are the laws about concealing weapons on one's person or in one's car?

John was about to ask whether carrying a weapon out in the open would be allowed if the weapon were loaded, when the tour moved off to the historical exhibits in the hallway. When John had clerked with the local public defender in law school, he once convinced a Superior Court judge that suspects arrested one night after tripping a silent alarm at a closed liquor store, had been detained without probable cause due to an overly broad description.

Then a public referendum was passed, loosening such police restrictions, and John's stint with criminal law ended.

The descriptions of suspects given in the midnight briefing were equally broad. The real chance of catching someone seemed to be through the coincidence of a variety of factors: physical description, vehicle description, location, etc.

Then again there was the guy arrested in an intersection, waving a samurai sword menacingly, described in the briefing. There probably wouldn't be too many like him out that night.

John took a closer look at the poster on the wall. It showed six smashed vehicles with explanations like, 'I was smashed' and 'I was wasted'. Having lost a cousin that way back in South Dakota, John felt that message.

B. Day Two

John was a half-hour late because he relied on his memory for the intersection where the training center is located. Mary found the address in his briefcase and sent it by text. John had already passed the location three times by then.

Lt. Konn's lecture included an explanation of the color codes for police tension: white (A-OK); yellow (vigilant and observing); orange (alert, sensing a threat); and red (weapon drawn, finger on trigger at level 3 of 5, safety off).

Sgt. Barnett later added another color, black (hyper-vigilant, suspicious beyond measure).

The HRC commissioners continued their tour of the training facility. Sgt. Linden showed the training weapons and the protective gear. Sgt. Haws showed the room full of obsolete driving simulators, and led the tour through a taser training session using laser points rather than electric prongs.

A lesson repeated emphatically was to choose to deploy a weapon before the situation had gone critical. The San Jose' Police Department's training center was also the Regional Police Officer State Training (POST) center, the only training center in the state for training personnel to train other officers. Santa Clara County Sheriff's deputies were also trained there.

Back to the lecture room, Lt. Konn provided detail on what the FBI has tracked as injury to officers on duty. Forty-four had been killed in combat with criminals throughout the country in 2007 (up from thirty-six that time last year).

Forty-two of those deaths involved firearms. Fifty-one had been killed accidentally across the country by this time in 2007; the previous year the total was forty-seven at that time of year.

The combat deaths ranged from traffic stops (most frequent) to drug-related incident. Twenty-three involved officers using protective vests. The accidental deaths were heaviest (twenty-eight) in the south, and ran from vehicle accidents to an allergic reaction to a bee sting.

Barnett takes us through the story of a foot pursuit he made on the East side. Later, Haws would do the same thing, concluding with a rendition of his hospital interview with the injured suspect. *"Why'd you run?"; "It was stupid, really dumb."*

Barnett lists the brain as the officer's best weapon. To be functional, it has to rely on common sense, good judgment, and sound decision-making. Close beyond that is the officer's fitness.

Safety should be first in the officer's mind. As a public servant, the priority is supposed to be the safety of the civilians (victims, witnesses, bystanders), followed by that of the officer. However, a dead officer never saved or helped anyone. So, the officer's own safety has to be primary.

Last on the list of the priorities for safety is the suspect, the perpetrator, the 'bad guy'. He goes into a story about Al Qaeda operatives who took over a school in Russia, and punctuates it with, "I hope nothing like that ever happens in America." He didn't account for Virginia Tech and Colorado slipped his mind, maybe because they involved domestic terrorists.

John drew a diagram of the preferred locations to position officers if trying to put an immobile school bus commandeered by kidnappers under arrest. He thought that the rear of the bus would be the most difficult to cover.

Films were shown that were taken from the patrol cars of officers who lost their lives in car stops that went bad. The point is well made. If an officer drops the guard, lets the situation escalate, or loses control, he or she can become a victim. In the classroom, John again thought of Virginia Tech and tried to imagine how to work one's way toward the shooter as others were diving for cover.

Panic became the next topic of discussion. The definition of 'crazy', that it involves doing the same thing over and over again, expecting a different result to arise, is offered.

Sgt. Barnett told how his weapon had misfired twice while doing room-to-room reconnaissance. His training had kicked in, enabling him to fall back twice while his accompanying officer stepped up. He blamed the gun's malfunction on improper cleaning after using it in training.

Each time the gun jammed, Barnett said that his mind thought, "That's interesting." It's an intrusive thought that has to be avoided in a crisis situation. A successful pattern in this situation would be 'move', 'communicate', 'shoot', or 'find cover'.

The officers and the commissioners discussed proper communication. Film of an LAPD incident involving two officers whose collar of a perp turned into a wrestling match with him getting a hand on one of their guns followed.

When the officer yelled "He's got my gun," Barnett explained, "When you hear that, it means to the officer's back-up to 'Shoot him'."

The sergeant explained that when the case went to court, the perp was exonerated because the officers had used the 'f-word' during the collar. This suggested to the jury that they had lost control of the situation and the perp was the one on the defensive.

Sgt. Ian Cooley took over and discussed the FBI's profile of the officer most likely to get hurt in the line of duty. The unfortunate one is likely to be one who tends to use less force than is necessary to control a situation, one who is taken off guard, and one who is 'service-oriented'.

The moral here is "Be ready for war," and "Good people love us, bad people hate me."

A survey is cited, in which two-thirds of the offenders moralized, "The officer didn't realize how serious the situation had become."

Red flags for danger are when the subject is uncooperative, and when he or she fails to follow instructions from the officer. Penal Code 148 allows an officer to use reasonable force for a person's failure to obey one of his orders.

Reasonable force at the lowest level can mean using the baton and handcuffs.

Sgt. Cooley conceded the point that he cannot know if the subject is developmentally disabled. He says, however, that one gets three-quarters of a second to identify activity as dangerous, and three-quarters of a second to react to it.

Hyper-vigilance can cause tunnel vision, auditory exclusion (the hearing shuts down), and solitary focus. Reasonable force has to be the response, until the threat dissipates (activity is no longer perceived as a threat).

Looking for a response from the party with whom the officer is engaged may result in the officer getting shot in the face. That was clearly the message from the films of the officers shot and killed, shown earlier in the evening.

Although, an example is given from one of the movies, regarding the exact time when the officer should have called for back-up, the advice is generally to "Solve the problem in front of you first; getting a radio will get you hurt."

Lt. Konn reminds the commissioners that in San Jose, exactly this time of year, an officer killing took place some years back, when Officer Fontana, two weeks out of the police academy, was shot in the face making a traffic stop.

(The slogans 'Anticipate, don't wait' and 'pre-incident management' are used synonymously.)

An interview with gang members was shown on film. One coldly explained that he has the advantage when the officer is poking his head into the car window.

He doesn't want to wait until the rest of the police force shows up. He wants to take that officer out 'right now'. Gang missions have become so outcome-oriented, that those involved may face a worse fate if they return to prison without having accomplished their mission, than they would expect from the law enforcement officer if they faced him or her down.

Of the officers' deaths caused by guns, 69% involved handguns; 49% of them were from a range of 0 to 5 feet; 12% more were from a distance of 11 to 20 feet.

John and the others left the lecture room for the spartanly equipped practice room with wrestling mat and punching bag. When given the opportunity, he whacked the bag three times with a baton, feeling relieved for the next day or two. At 56, John's hitting the thing without landing on the floor was a moral victory.

Lt. Konn closes with the story of how the flesh was ripped off the back of his hand when he collared a woman's husband at a restaurant. He learned something about himself then—that he could hit a woman.

C. Day Three

The session began with the introduction of three officers trained in anti-terrorism techniques. It quickly shifted focus to questions raised by email to Lt. Konn, who explained that when an officer becomes involved in an altercation on an encounter with a civilian, another officer takes the culprit to the department for booking. This is to prevent encounters from escalating uncontrollably.

Sgt. Brett Linden discussed 'stress inoculation', i.e., the training in controlling emotions. The class wasn't satisfied. What about an emergency situation where a language other than English is involved?

Lt. Konn explained that AT&T Communication Services available through the patrol's cell phones were for providing an interpretation of languages when an officer isn't available for onsite translation.

John asked about the situation where one officer witnesses another officer using unnecessary force (e.g., hitting a person with a baton when the person has already submitted to authority and is being compliant).

Lt. Konn responded that officers are trained to intercede in such situations. This may include calling a medical response team.

Sgt. Haws added that police training includes a legal, ethical component, regarding reporting misconduct of fellow officers in the field.

Sgt. Barnett added that the police academy's class in the use of force includes a force-option simulator, nineteen hours of training on the SJPD force policy, case law regarding police use of force and other things.

This is 'reinforced' with four hours per week of training on physical skills, over the course of twenty weeks.

Capt. Kirby sensed that John was not satisfied with the answers to his question about the protocol for reporting misconduct witnessed by a fellow officer. Kirby brought up the Rodney King incident.

Kirby explained that when a supervisor is suspected of hiding an incident or mischaracterizing it, the chain of reporting on that incident is 'realigned'.

The management of the review is handled as the investigation of a potential criminal violation in itself.

To conclude, John asked about the Duty Manual and whether it contains a policy against one officer retaliating against another when a report has been filed regarding potential police misconduct. Kirby confirmed that there is such a written policy.

Sgt. Barnett responded to a question about the eventuality of an officer getting injured on the job. At that time, statistically, a police officer was killed in the line of duty once every fifty-two hours.

Nonetheless, there's no force used in 97% of the arrests. The tactics, techniques and procedures designed to prevent situations from escalating may nevertheless make it look, from a distance, as if the officer is over-reacting to minor stimuli.

The officers also asked for consideration for the officer who has to sleep in his car so that he or she can testify in court early the next morning after working the graveyard shift.

Even trained professionals may suffer from 'frayed nerves' under conditions of being unable to return home for thirty-six hours due to a combination of these factors.

Capt. Kirby explained how he sizes up a person encountered in his rounds. Physically, the person may seem normal but various signs may indicate a mental imbalance. Tattoos may be covers for heroin tracks.

Burns may indicate crack or meth use. When an officer engages a suspect in battle, the civilian's temperature may rise so high that it becomes life threatening.

Some war stories about hand-to-hand combat in San Jose' follow. They segue into discussion of detentions, arrests, warrants, searches, and seizures.

Sgt. Haws led the discussion through a 61-page reading assignment by asking pointed questions and eliciting vague recollections from non-professionals.

Haws qualified as an expert in court regarding signs of suspect intoxication and appropriate officer response.

On the subject of citizen tips to law enforcement, anonymous or otherwise, Capt. Kirby spoke of the crime stoppers hotline, the narcotics info hotline, and the gang info hotline.

With the first of these, a caller gets a specific investigation number and detail regarding potential rewards.

With the database and methods for accessing various info banks, even the most minute information can be very valuable to an investigation.

Haws showed videos of actual and recreated incidents where a stop was justified and the driver refused to cooperate, resulting in his arrest. 'Arrest' is defined as requiring physical restraint or submission to custody.

John asked whether an arrest has been effected if an officer knocks a person out.

Sgt. Haws said that it depends upon the subject's subjective notion of whether he's free to leave or not, although a pre-arrest detention might give the subject the same impression.

In the officer's mind, the key considerations are whether a subject is cooperating with investigatory questioning or violating a law that would impede the officer from performing his duty.

But if the subject refuses to take a field sobriety test, the officer may take him or her into custody and search the passenger compartment of the vehicle or the area immediately surrounding the person in a building.

Still skeptical, John asked about preservation of evidence. "Isn't it selective—the evidence potentially exonerating the suspect is ignored or not retrieved, but the evidence inculpating him or her is preserved?" He queried.

Capt. Kirby explained that the cops responding to a call do not do the crime scene investigation. They apprehend the person and take evidence immediately available, but detectives respond to the scene to do a fuller investigation.

John asked about removal of others present, so that the scene cannot be adjusted in the interim, before the detectives have arrived. He's told it depends on the situation.

After Sgt. Leanno Fonsley gave a demonstration of a police encounter responding to a call regarding domestic violence, he gave written material regarding such matters.

SJPD policy is that police responding to such reports do so in pairs, never by one officer alone. There usually are follow-up interviews and channeling to counseling, but once a complaint has been made, an arrest is mandatory.

The most common domestic violence victim is a female between 16 and 24 years old.

There followed a hands-on exposition of a car stop on reasonable cause, frisk of suspect, search of the vehicle, and pre-arrest interrogation. At the end was a concealed weapon, a sword hidden inside the suspect's cane; and a kit for cutting and snorting coke had gone undetected.

The suspect's belt is examined, revealing a detachment that breaks into an ugly brass knife.

D. Day Four

An officer in Southern California responded to a call and found a guy in the middle of an intersection wielding a knife. The officer suspected that he was drunk or high, told him to drop the knife, and then directed him to get on his knees.

An arm's length from the weapon, he drew it to stab the officer on his approach. The cop went to trial for excessive force when he took the suspect out with a handgun.

The theory of the lawyer who took the case for municipality liability was that the officer could have tried lesser force to take the suspect into custody. The court found that the officer only needed a reasonable belief that he was being exposed to serious bodily injury when he reacted by use of deadly force.

That belief was based on what the officer knew at the time of the action, including reports that he may rely upon, whether right or wrong, or whether superseded by later events.

The officer may have known what he was doing but he made an error in judgment. Cops have to defend themselves in lawsuits even though they are immunized by statute.

John saw a movie in which an officer is rendering aid to a shot victim on the ground, and then is assaulted by the victim's brother on PCP, who arrived late and just thought that the cop was the one who put his brother down.

The smaller officer is thrown against a salad bar sneeze guard, picked up and slammed against a grating covering the front door. Then he was thrown onto the windshield of a compact in the parking lot.

The officer's partner arrived and misapplied a carotid restraint from behind.

The cop who had been slammed around was eventually sued on the theory that he shouldn't have tried to use his baton and flashlight to ward off the attacker. The court dismissed the action.

In a simulator room, the star HRC commissioner with the degree in criminal justice is quickly plugged when he can't get his revolver out of the holster in time to avoid getting shot by the smaller woman in a group. His tunnel vision had concentrated on the unarmed large man.

The sprightly small older woman from the Chaplain's office does much better in defending herself. The black woman from the County Social Services Office does even better, until she freezes when it's time to close in on the suspect and he's on her before she can stop him.

Then the middle-aged man from the County Human Relations Office was confronted by a fellow who walked menacingly toward him. He drew his pepper spray adeptly, but had trouble getting the nozzle deployed and pointed in the right direction.

Eventually, he got two shots off, both missed the culprit badly. The third try, probably too late in real life, blasted the bad guy directly in the face.

John is told by the instructor that he and his partner should go into the dark house with the open front door, guns drawn. The report from a neighbor was that this house is occupied by a single woman who never left her door open and who always kept her lights on. Both of these are different on approach.

John's partner flashed the light from corner to corner as they passed through the family room adjoining the kitchen. Nothing there.

In the den, the only suspicious thing in the total darkness was a window open with its screen intact.

John called out for the occupants to come out where they can be seen.

Just then, they hear a scream from an apparent female victim. John called dispatch for a 'Code 3 fill' (back-up), and yelled to the assailant, "Leave her alone. Step away from her."

Half-way up the stairs, the victim yelled, "He's raping me!" John screamed for him to leave her alone.

John and partner step into the bedroom. Two figures are prostrate on the bed. The one on top was wriggling to maintain control. John watched the movements while telling him to get out of the bed.

When the assailant finally rose up, John saw a knife in his right hand. His partner yelled, "He's got a knife."

John responded, "Roger that."

After several futile efforts to talk the guy into dropping the weapon, he started toward John. He failed to comply when John told him to stand facing the wall. John had just enough time to fire off a round before the screen froze.

The training officer asked John, "Why did you put your left hand back on top of the weapon after I told you not to do that?"

He answered, "I was anticipating the gun's recoil, and I wanted to keep a level barrel," was not accepted, because the instructor said that these guns don't have much of a backfire.

The screen showed that John hit the criminal with a shot below the waist. "Why did you aim low?"

John had thought he had hit him dead center in the chest, but responded, "I wanted to avoid the risk of missing the guy entirely and hitting the victim in the background."

A replay of the shooting on tape showed that the woman had sat up in her bed and was within 45 degrees from the attacker's heart.

The instructor asked, "Would that single shot in the leg have stopped the guy?"

John replied, "Not at all."

His next question was, "What would you do next? I saw you put the gun back into your holster. I saw you put the strap back over the gun after you did so. Did you think it was over?"

"No," John answered. "I put the gun in the holster because I wanted that hand free of encumbrances."

The instructor asked, "You were anticipating hand-to-hand combat?"

John said, "Yes. And if the gun got free of my holster, there was a 50-50 chance that it would be used against me."

"So how are you going to handle the attacker after your gun is out of play?"

"Well, I use the attacker's momentum to sidestep him, twist his arm, flip him, and subdue him when he's on the ground," John replied. John wasn't asked to demonstrate.

The instructor wanted to know if that's 'guaranteed to work'. "No," John answered. "I could get stabbed. It's all a matter of probability."

The instructor informed the class that he has seen 'lots of dead bodies'. This is too much for the lady from the County Human Relations Department, who collapsed. Paramedics were called and the class was dismissed.

E. Day Five

After about three hours of lectures on the benefits, wonders, and usefulness of the taser stun gun with barbed ends that fly from a hand-held weapon and shoot electricity into a person when pulling the trigger at the other end, John and company were marched into a room with wrestling mat for a floor, and presented with the thrill of shooting such a weapon into an aluminum-foil-covered mock-up with a male person's outline of head, torso and frame.

But first they were offered the luxury of being subjects of a taser-shooting of their own. One of the brave HRC commissioners volunteers mysteriously, and the others watched him writhe on the mat as voltage was run into the back of his upper thigh for about three seconds.

John wondered at the excitement. Others from the group stepped forward, including one female who wanted to stand up for her gender when the instructor pleaded, "We need at least one woman to try it!"

John wasn't sure of the logic behind the plea for gender equality, especially since the effects are demonstrated on the application not to be any different for a female than they are for a male.

Then when there are no more volunteers, the instructor felt compelled to call John out by name—to ask him to try it. That was evidently a perk of his status as chair of the HRC.

The police officers took a sadistic thrill from shooting the liberals and other community stalwarts with the electric weapon not unlike a cattle prod (except for the tethers that allow it to reach a target 15 feet away with accuracy).

John declined politely. He had been convinced that the weapon does as described, both from the videotape produced by the manufacturer and from observing others get tased in his presence.

Calculating the pros and cons of his stepping up as a guinea pig, John estimated his anatomy to be no more resilient to such current than that of the 6'5" 300-lb. guy who had gone before him.

Also, when he had signed his release of the SJPD from liability for personal injury before starting this academy,

John had specifically lined out the part about consenting to be the target of a taser discharge; he did the city a favor by not proceeding with the shock and then suing them afterward for exceeding the scope of his limited release.

When the demonstration was finished, and each had been given the opportunity to see the remarkable weapon, they were dismissed and told to return on Saturday, 3 November, for a cop car driving session.

F. Day Six

This was truly a day in the life of a police cadet. Starting off with coffee at the training center, chatting with a large, pony-tailed white truck driver and a smallish, black female HRC member, John committed the faux pas of answering a question about the contents of his hand-bag, with a response, "Gatorade and my watermelon."

John was trying to explain the bulkiness of the bag.

Then they were transported to the driving site where police officers were trained in managing their vehicles. The most impressive thing about the car itself was the ABS (anti-lock braking system), that enables the turning of the car while the brakes are being applied full-force.

This prevents rear-enders in close situations, although he was told that they still occur.

Inside the car, John was treated to reverse 180 degree turns. He's glad he had his flack-jacket on. The Spartan furnishings of the backseat of a patrol car do not include cushions. Bare-metal frame seating without padding on the sides or armrests make for an uncomfortable ride.

John surmised that the stripped-down interior was to discourage riders from coming back.

In a moment of self-revelation after the officers have demonstrated how to drive this beast, and after they had taken their turns at the wheel, John declined the opportunity to take a leak in the men's room with the gay HRC member.

John took the wheel of a cruiser to trace a car serving as an escape vehicle, with another car providing interference every so often. This simulates the street traffic encountered in a car chase with the siren on. John went tunnel-vision and locked in on following as closely as possible to the 'rabbit'.

He was tagged with four near-collisions with the interference car.

John's time behind the wheel ended when the interference car was clearly at the intersection before him. John slammed on his brakes, turned his wheels right, and slid to a stop.

The interference car stopped, too, enabling John to resume the chase. With the wheels turned sharply to the right, he couldn't just gun it and straighten out in time to make the turn into the chase lane.

John knocked over a pylon on the left and took out three more on the right. He realized that he was reenacting the 'crash and burn' scenarios from the video games that played with his kids, in which they, like this training officer, took the controls.

After lunch, at the firing range with real-life deadly weapons, John tested an 11-round single barrel shotgun, a rifle, a high-powered assault gun, .38 and 9-millimeter handguns, and a 44-millimeter stun gun that fires hard-rubber balls. He hit all the targets but one.

In trying to load the shotgun, he dropped one cartridge and the instructor gingerly held the barrel of his weapon while reaching down to get it.

The safeties were always on before shooting and the barrels and chambers were checked by the person firing and another observer, before being taken down.

The commissioners were told of the time in 1993 when the trainer confronted a guy under the influence of methamphetamines in downtown San Jose. He was waving shears and threatening people at random.

The officer parked his car in response to the call about a block away. While trying to get his seatbelt off and get out of the vehicle, the suspect ran upon his car but swerved away at the same time.

The officer was thinking of the progression of force to which he was entitled, as the offender ignored the application of OC-spray, warded off two baton blows and took off running again.

The officer needed to use his gun when the guy tried to attack him with the shears. Between him and the officer who came up behind him, the suspect was hit eight times, once in the heart.

Even after the firing stopped, he was still rearing up to strike the cop, although he died before he could reach him.

This officer spent two and one-half years thereafter, defending a lawsuit that went to a 3-week jury trial regarding his use of force.

The time from parking his car to cessation of gun shots, reported by radio, had only been 35 seconds. The plaintiff's expert was given thirty-six hours to review the evidence taken in at the trial before he testified.

The expert's ultimate opinion was that the officer used too much OC-spray, allowing some of the extended application to wash earlier-applied spray from the culprit's eyes. The jury found for the officer and the police department.

The officer said that, of the equipment that had come on-line since this 1993 incident, the new weapon that would have been most effective in dealing with this situation was the taser, but that wasn't guaranteed.

People have taken the taser barbs out of their chest, immediately after they landed. When an officer was chasing someone, one barb could strike and stick, but another might miss or bounce off.

Throwing the taser down is not the officer's best solution. He suggested taking the attachment for the deployed tasers out of the gun, installing an attachment with new set of barbs, and firing again when in position.

G. Day Seven

The commissioners were treated to a dinner of lasagna, roast chicken, mixed salad, Italian bread with cheese spread, some vegetable assortment and slices of cheesecake. They went by van to the abandoned City Hall building on Mission Street and were fitted for holsters and bulletproof vests.

At the meeting room, they were given a refresher on handling the Glock, including loading, reloading, aiming, etc. Sgt. Ian Cooley gave a lecture on tactics in clearing buildings of suspects, on a room-by-room sweep with at least one partner.

The commissioners practiced peering around the corners of the building's darkened interior, trying to get full view of cardboard suspects (including Osama) without giving up full vantages of themselves.

Then they walked into a room with framed mock interior rooms with targets posted on the walls. On sight of geometric shapes, they were supposed to fire blanks from their modified Glocks.

The parties went through two-by-two, some demonstrating surprising agility and dexterity in coordinating sweeps back-to-back.

On John's turn, he was paired with the aggression averse lady who had barely been able to muster the gumption to budge a punching bag with her baton. She was the same one who had collapsed the night of our simulated rescue.

Midway through the exercise, John noted that she had become even less aggressive in her movements, perhaps deferring to him. John was guarding the rear. She knew that evil would be lurking around the corner they were nearing.

John nudged her out with his rear end. Before breathing again, John spied yellow tilted squares on the wall in the opposite room. He aimed and fired, taking out each one, one at a time.

John's gun jammed. In real life, he may have nailed the targets on first encounter. If not, he would have been toast.

Instructor Barnett tried to clear the jam in his revolver. John said, "Man, I am sooo dead." Barnett rebuked him for 'negative death humor', something that was unwelcome on this range.

On the way out of the building, John asked Barnett, "Don't you find that some partners are more compatible with one another than others, in this kind of exercise?"

"Yes," he answered, adding that, "Some people can anticipate each other's actions better than others can."

The commanding officer in charge of the exercise was disappointed because the trainees had spent so much time on the lecture and early drills, leaving little time for simulated moving targets. To make matters worse, they had spent their ammo shooting at cardboard mock-ups.

Three officers were waiting in the wings, ready to serve as real-life experience of moving from room to room in unknown surroundings danger behind every door.

H. Day Eight

The news came out that the FBI's annual rankings of the safest cities in the U.S., with populations over 500,000, placed San Jose' as the third-safest, behind Honolulu and El Paso, but ahead of New York City. SJPD had maintained no. 1 position for six years.

The commissioners were broken into two groups again. Fitted with bullet-proof vests and holsters again, they went into a storage room for helmets, neck and groin protectors, and modified handguns.

Broken down into groups first of two, and later of four, the trainers gave them scenarios to involve live confrontations with officers as combatants or victims.

One of those in the second group promptly shot a mother cradling a baby doll in her arms; the wound on her thigh would be lethal if left unattended.

At the prompting of Officer Lindley, John applied direct pressure after dragging her out of the line of fire. At her desperate urging, he returned to the live-fire room to pick up the doll posing as a baby and got it out of the line of live shooters.

John looked around to see that two of the four in his group were gone. One of them had run out of ammo and was shot; another's gun had jammed and he had just retreated out of sight.

John could have used those guys to assist with medical treatment. He had to step up to take the place of shooter no. 2. As he did, he saw an officer on the ground in need of assistance.

John didn't recognize the partner from his group. He insisted that he push his gun down on the floor before he would go in.

John kicked the gun out of the way and began to drag the officer out, calling out for cover and keeping his gun hand pointed down the hall.

No one confronted him until after he got his partner to safety.

Then John had to go down the hall. The room to the right looked safe, and when his partner asked if it's cleared, he told him to double-check. John's partner later told him that he found a live, armed suspect in the closet.

Turning the corner to the left, John saw the silhouette of a 6 feet tall man in the left corner. He barked commands to him while pointing the pistol in his direction. The subject didn't respond.

John told him to drop his gun and put his hands up.

Still no response. John wasn't going to fire at him until he was sure what he's doing. The guy might just be a confused, uninvolved spectator. Or he could be no. 1 in the bad-guy chain of command.

John braced his arm against the wall at the doorway and decided to freeze the situation until the other guy moved, complied, started firing, or else back-up for John arrived.

Then the exercise was called off. The commissioners and trainers tried to analyze what happened. Lt. Konn praised John for dragging him out.

Their next exercise involved confronting a man sitting on a sofa with a gun pointed toward his head. John talked him into dropping the gun and moved in to secure him.

Then he realized that this guy's brother, whom the suicide-threatening guy blamed as being the source his problems, was armed and dangerous.

John had innocently commanded the brother to go down the hallway and get out of his sight or else be arrested. The brother left, wandered back down the hallway, carrying a concealed weapon.

John passed the brother off to his partner for processing, but she was reluctant and unaware of what to do. She said, "Thanks a lot."

John's partner hadn't seen either John's move or the brother's threat coming. John's tunnel-vision on the suicide-threat had left his partner in lethal danger.

The recruits next go into a room for instructions on the art of using a baton to take out an unarmed combatant. After some drilling with a punching bag, they were sent to fight an academy instructor wearing protective armor.

The instructor took live swings at the recruits and tried to butt them off their feet.

Some of the commissioners lost their batons but the instructor congenially allowed them to retrieve them, before rejoining the fight.

The next day, John was sore in the upper arms from giving a straight-arm to the instructor, fending him off. This enabled John to crank a good, hard swing with the baton from his side.

The instructor charged John, who turned the baton sideways, butting him with its end. This stopped the instructor short. John then used the baton as a bar to prevent him from advancing.

Far and away his most effective use of the baton was a baseball-bat swing that, as a former switch-hitter, he can make equally from either side.

When a few of his swings go awry and hit the instructor squarely on his helmet, the group was later told that police policy was that as long as John wasn't swinging deliberately for the head, that would be OK.

Blows that glance off the suspect's shoulders and hit him on the neck or head were permitted by official policy. This also applied to groin shots, but John wasn't awkward enough to land any of those.

In a match with the tallest and heaviest guy in their class, John and his group went back in to take control of an armed instructor. Having tried earlier with a female classmate to run the bad guy into a wall, only to run the suspect directly into his partner, John learned that he can't always anticipate where his partner is going to be.

This time, they had the bad guy cornered with John's tall, heavy partner off to his right. He logically took the route that he thought would encounter the least resistance.

John let him have it across the chest with a lightweight baton. Then as he diverted toward his partner, John hit him again with a glancing blow on his right rib-cage.

The instructor stumbled in between John and his partner. John realized that his partner wasn't going after him.

John crowded the instructor from behind and then pushed him down. Once he was on the ground, John fell on top of him to keep him from getting up again.

That exercise was over. John left the training center to tell Mary the story, but she just yawned and went to bed.

I. Last Day, Day Nine

The academy lived up to its billing as providing the ultimate in gore and blood. The sergeant managing six officers in the SJPD Homicide Division showed slides of photos taken at three crime scenes. They weren't as tidy as the ones on television; real criminals aren't as neat.

There was a chopped-up body in a freezer (patricide) from a Santa Teresa High School 'F' student. There was a decayed corpse wrapped in a sleeping bag for months below an old car in the garage while garbage piled up on the sides, found to be part of a spousal shooting.

There was a juvenile chopped up with a meat cleaver as an execution by a neighborhood gang.

The stories supported the rule that the perpetrator ordinarily returns to the scene of the crime. In two of them, the perpetrator continued to live in the house where he had committed the murder.

Hiding the bodies on site wasn't a model criminal cover-up. Their methods didn't include using bleach to try to eliminate blood stains. These scenarios predated more common use of DNA evidence for identification.

In the parking lot outside the training facility, the commissioners toured vehicles used by the SWAT team as stations for their operations in hostage situations. They saw rifles with scopes, calculators that help the sniper adjust for wind and temperature, and range finders for estimating distance to targets.

Officer Jiménez disclosed detail on why a sniper would use camouflage in an urban setting.

The commissioners saw the vehicle used to approach a barricaded culprit occasionally. Constructed like a HUMMER, it is heavier and probably rides like a tank. Like the vehicles seen on television, it has benches on both sides toward the rear.

The ammunition and supply van was less sturdy, although its cartridges and other ammo were locked up in cabinets inside. There was rope, other combat supplies, a computer, and a fax machine inside. These enabled communications with the officers in the station.

The commanding officer gave a short discourse on military history, drawn from his experience with the Army, starting a month before the Tet offensive. He had been part of the division that 'took back Hue' within the first six months of his service in the Vietnam War.

This officer was no-nonsense. John mentioned a reenactment on television where the 'bad guy' had been surrounded but nevertheless was itching to get away. In that situation, the officer in command had authorized a shooter with a 'less lethal' weapon to take one shot before the other officers would fire.

The gunman saved a life by hitting his target with the less-lethal weapon on two shots, allowing the suspect to be taken into custody.

One of the officers regularly assigned to hostage situations said that fatigue can become a factor when officers are on a siege outside a barricaded structure. The officers on the scene should have adequate food and rest, to make reliable decisions and execute them reliably.

Police in hostage situations try to keep the culprit busy with negotiations. Culprits who have been thus occupied tend not to be as ready to defend themselves when the assault begins.

Suspects in hostage situations don't usually ask for or get food and drink. Probably they would assume that such nourishment would be spiked or drugged to give the police officers an advantage in ensuing altercations.

John and the others were next given the opportunity to speak about their experience at the academy. John told of the running joke with Mary whenever approaching a scene where an officer has pulled someone over, he would ask her, "Should we stop and render assistance?"

The officers received this story with apprehension as the joke could turn south easily. John elaborated, "My wife is never very keen on that idea." The crowd met that with tepid, nervous laughter.

John added, "Uncertain how receptive the officer would be to my offer..." met with uproarious laughter, which increased when John added, "...especially if they know me."

John continued, "This training reminded me of the situation in my neighborhood where two officers came to my door, asking questions about the guy who lived next door to me. I didn't know at the time but he was a fugitive."

"We had this curious conversation in which they were politely and courteously getting what little information I had, but at the same time, were obviously sizing me up as a potential suspect."

"Maybe I was feeding them bad information, maybe I was not telling them everything I knew, maybe I was even harboring the guy," John explained.

John went on, "When the conversation was over, I thought to myself, '*Those guys must be schizophrenic.*'"

John finished with, "But now, as a result of this program, I understand the two sides of the line you people have to walk to do your jobs effectively. Maybe next time I won't be so hard on the law enforcement officers."

As John stepped down, Lt. Konn mentioned that the officers were impressed with his tactics in the exercises, particularly in the rooms involving active shooters.

Barnett chimed in, that "The red man (training officer in armored suit) is still recuperating from his baton work." This gave John the turn to laugh nervously.

Later on, when the trainers were given their chance to evaluate the commissioners, Barnettp said, "Don't be hesitant to join in when you see a law enforcement officer having trouble with a suspect. Just grab a baton and start right in."

The SWAT team exposition showed John that even in his sleepy town of one million plus, this type of equipment was available for rare emergencies.

Since recreational use of pot was not yet legal, he learned that its growers were often relieved to learn that the people breaking down their doors and entering hostilely weren't always competitors, but sometimes 'Just the police'.

There was less chance of getting shot that way.

Chapter 29
27 January 2021,
10:00 o'clock Adventure

Realizing he didn't have enough to hold John longer, and in hopes that he could get him back for good if he let him go now, the Devil released John's spirit, thinking to himself, *He'll be back.*

When John came around, he was staring up at the lights on the undertaker's examining table. He coughed a bit and then spit up some blood.

Startled, the undertaker turned around and looked at him as if he were seeing a ghost.

"We thought you were gone, John," he said.

"Where am I?" John asked.

Mary was taking Miles and Sasha for a walk, when the thought occurred to her that John's phone hadn't been recovered. She went back to the spot where they had found him and found it.

She took it to the police department. Sure enough, John had managed to turn his video recorder on and it stayed on until the battery expired. Maybe this would help to find the culprits.

Mary returned to her house and took the dogs for a walk. To her surprise, as they approached the street, Sasha wanted to cross it despite the darkness on the other side.

Sasha was usually more adventurous than Miles, so that seemed to be logical. The snow that had fallen earlier in the day was now beaten into the ground to form a sheer, slippery coating on the road, almost as slick as ice.

The dogs didn't have trouble getting across, but Mary quickly became aware that she should be careful. Her footing wasn't as sure as theirs.

Twice when they reached the other side of the road, Mary learned this lesson the hard way. She slipped twice, once on her back and another time to her side, both times hitting the ground heavily, and holding onto the dogs' leashes only by sheer determination.

Thinking that the path being chosen by Sasha couldn't be much worse, Mary and Miles followed her onto a walkway that had been only partly cleared of snow earlier.

The path was obviously cut by a snowblower but it had not reached near the surface of the pavement. Instead, there was a nice, clean-cut incision in the snow about 25 inches deep, leaving about 15 inches of packed snow above the surface.

This was enough for Mary to navigate confidently, until her boots started to sink into the snow from place to place, even as she avoided stepping into footprints left by other walkers before her.

Twice Mary lurched to the side, nearly falling into the snowbank on her right, as her boots cut deep into what was left on the ground before her. She saw the path cut clearly.

She determined from its direction that it would lead to the bridge over a creek ahead about a half mile, just enough distance for them to divert to the road near-by and return by that route.

Mary had managed to let Sasha lead them by the 20 feet on her leash, but Miles's lack of interest in following this route had convinced him to stay immediately behind Mary, on a shorter leash.

Miles almost tripped Mary as he pressed forward when Mary was finding the footing treacherous, but she managed to keep him from passing her on the snow-packed path.

The trek continued as the dusk gathered and Mary was reassured to see cars traveling on the road to her left about 75 to a 100 yards away. There was no snow falling, but the moon allowed enough reflection off the snow for her to see where they were going.

As they neared the bridge, Mary was glad to see that the path did indeed run through the undeveloped land directly to the bridge built for foot-traffic and bicyclists.

Usually, the dogs would try to go one direction or another, other than the direction Mary wanted them to go, so that they could sniff various bushes, shrubs, and bare ground. Mary would have to tug the leashes back to get them going her way.

But that was not the way this walk was progressing. The snow on each side of the path was too high for the dogs to leave it, although from time to time, they found something of enough interest to stop and sniff.

Still Sasha maintained a long distance before them and Miles was close to Mary.

After passing over the bridge, Mary became aware that the road was bending farther to her left. The pathway had not taken them toward the road when they reached the other side of the bridge.

The path was still cut as reliably clean as before, although to Mary's consternation, there was still enough loosely-packed snow below her feet for her to stumble more regularly than before.

Once or twice, Mary fell to her knees, and once even to her forearms, as she found the footing more difficult. Once or twice, she felt like the burden of losing John was too much to make rising from the cold ground where she could pass peacefully to the afterlife.

If for no other reason, Mary rose to her feet each time for fear that the dogs wouldn't make it home safely without her.

Getting up became more difficult each time. Still the thought occurred to her that if she didn't get up, she would pass painlessly, as freezing to death is one of the least painful ways to go.

She fought off the temptation and cussed herself for being self-piteous.

Mary realized that the dogs wouldn't survive the night if they were tied to her by the leashes, and that they wouldn't leave her no matter how lifeless her body had become.

Miles and Sasha were in a path seldom traveled at night. The cars on the road were too far away to see them, and those who could were too focused on their personal business to notice them. Things were not looking good for the threesome.

As Mary rose to her feet, a car pulled up on a side-access road and stopped before her. Miles and Sasha began to growl. Sasha started barking. Miles was standing reliably near Mary but growing apprehensive.

Now the lighting was getting worse, the cars passing on the road were becoming more infrequent, and the moon was partially covered by clouds gathering from the west.

Mary thought about waving to passing cars but realized that none of them had paid any attention before, and probably none of them would heed a call now either.

Mary was becoming chilled, although her jacket was strong enough to keep her warm.

As two men got out of the vehicle, Mary reached a decision. Since the path cut by the snowblower was not bending way from the road, she was past the bridge without a pathway to the road.

The only things in the direction she was going were a maintenance shed for the Forestry Department and an open field that led to the back of a residential area.

She decided to cut across the heavy snow toward the road. The men were headed in her direction, but they hesitated when they saw where she was going.

"This will be easy enough," said one to the other.

"Yeah, fetch the rope," said the other.

As Mary waded through snow that was mid-thigh in height, she held the leashes but the dogs were hesitant to follow. Her legs opened up a partial walkway that would have been enough for a teenager to follow him, but the dogs were right to hesitate.

As luck would have it, when cutting into the snowbank, Mary had dislodged part of the snow at the rugged corner she was cutting. The leashes oddly became stuck in that piece of snow.

Miles looked back and forth between this part of the snowbank and where Mary was standing. He couldn't have followed her if he wanted to.

Even if Miles had cleared the corner, the soft snow left by Mary's walking would still have been too much for him to traverse without difficulty. Sasha, being about half the size of Miles, wouldn't have made it across the 50 yards of deep, new snow to the road.

Mary returned to the corner where the leashes were stuck. The men by this time were almost upon her, one of them dangling a rope in his hand.

Realizing that the dogs wouldn't be going the way she wanted, Mary looked at the snowblower-cut path ahead of her and was convinced that she wouldn't make it past the men to get to the road.

There was no safety in the maintenance shed, the open field, or the residential area.

Mary thought of tying one dog up, carrying the other dog to the road, tying that dog up and returning to the first dog, but there wouldn't be enough time to get that done before the men got to her.

Her pant-legs were starting to feel wet from the snow she had cut through to this point.

The men rushed toward her, ignoring Miles and Sasha. Sasha started off back in the direction from which they came and Miles followed quickly.

Before their leashes were fully extended, Mary realized the wisdom of their suggestion and followed suit.

As she ran, Mary found that holding the leashes for both dogs provided a better three-point plane for her to maintain her balance, even as the dogs mutually pulled harder together than when Miles was at her feet and Sasha was 5 yards ahead.

Mary seldom lost her footing, and at length, they were at the slippery street when she had fallen before they took the snowblower-cut path. Mary was panting more heavily than the dogs at this point, but they knew enough not to cross the road in the same place where Mary had fallen before.

Mary scurried to the other side of the icy road and bent over to catch her breath. Just then, one of the men who had been chasing her rounded the corner and headed toward her.

Mary's pant-legs were soaking wet. She looked up to see the guy crossing the ice before her. Before she had a chance to decide how to defend herself, the guy had slipped on the ice, fell much harder than she had earlier, and hit his head on the ground with a terrific thud.

As she approached the man, she realized that he had been rendered unconscious and was out completely. Thinking fast, she took the dogs' leashes and tied him up.

Terrified that the other guy would be coming upon them soon, she scooped up some snow, packed it tight, and shoved it into the culprit's mouth, jamming it in so hard that he couldn't release it once he regained consciousness.

Once Miles and Sasha were released, they yelped loudly and ran off in the direction from which the bandit came, turned the corner and vanished.

Shortly after Mary finished tying her pursuer up and jamming the snowball into his mouth, she was preparing to defend herself against the other intruder. Much to her relief, she saw Miles and Sasha jumping back toward her, leaping nervously and joyfully.

Following the dogs came John, dragging the other bandit, whom he had taken by surprise and overcome.

In shocked amazement, she yelled, "Where did you come from?"

John replied, "I've been to hell and back!"

He explained that he had traced Mary's steps with the dogs in the snow, finding them not at home when the undertaker had taken him back.

After turning the bandits over to the police, when Mary disrobed for a shower, she found the skin of her legs, from the thighs to the shins, in patches of red on a background of white, suggesting that she was nearly frost-bitten.

John instantly took care of Miles and Sasha who were none the worse for wear.

Mary checked her Twitter for words of consolation. She found these prophetic words from the great American novelist Kurt Vonnegut: *A step backward, after making a wrong turn, is a step in the right direction.*